H.L. Swan

Dedication

Thank you for believing in me, Shura.

To my Wattpad readers; always slow dance while they scream.

"They had no past. They had no future. They just were."

-    Paullina Simons, The Bronze Horseman

One

A piercing ring blares through the speakers, jolting me from my daydream.

"Students! You've survived your first year of college. Congratulations and stay out of trou–" The professor's voice is drowned out by the loud cheers and rushed sounds of my fellow classmates hastily exiting the building as the last bell of the year chimes, signifying that it's the start of summer break.

I can't believe my first year in college has rolled by so quickly. I narrow my eyes as I scan the mass of moving bodies in the hallway, smiling when I spot a bobbing blonde bouncing my way.

Ashley nudges my arm. "Did you pass?"

"Finals? Thankfully, yes. I've done nothing but study. You?"

Rolling her eyes, she flips her hair over a slender

shoulder. "Don't wanna talk about it."

I laugh. I already know her grades are nothing but stellar.

Shoulder to shoulder, we make our way towards our freedom. The unusually warm Oregon air sweeps my chestnut hair across my face as we step through the propped open metal doors. The excitement is still palatable as we walk out of building C.

We're free! Well, for the summer anyways.

"I can't believe we are finished with our freshman year!" Ashley squeals, throwing her head back dramatically.

"I can't wait for tonight!" I exclaim happily.

I haven't seen Ian in a week, and I miss him so much. He's been so busy between Lacrosse and finals he just hasn't had the time. But tonight, I'm surprising him.

As though reading my thoughts, Ashley nudges my arm. "We know you're more excited to see Ian than anything." She fans herself.

I blush. It's true. My excitement isn't about the freedom I'll have for three months. Well, it is, but only because I get to spend all my time with Ian. We have been together for about two months now. It hasn't been very long, but he is so sweet to me, and handsome.

"Anyways," Ashley's lips curve into a half smile, redirecting me from my longing thoughts. "You know my brother is on his way here...right?"

"Yeah! I'm excited to meet more of your family. Your mom is the best!"

Ashley waves her hand in the air. "Just don't get

too excited. He's not the nicest person to be around."

"I can handle a mean brother. We're practically sisters. He has to be nice to me."

Her eyes widen slightly, "I'm his sister and he's not even nice to me. Well, he's okay, I guess." She fixes her previous statement.

"It'll be fun," I say absentmindedly, my thoughts on what to wear later.

There's a party at the frat house for the beginning of summer and I want to look my best, especially since I know how much Ian hates surprises, so I need to make up for it by looking cute. He thinks I'm going to my mom's for the weekend, but I wanted to make tonight special.

We hop into my Altima and roll the windows down, enjoying the breeze that overtakes the car as we drive away from the prison we pay to go to.

Freshmen usually live in the dorms, but when I met Ash on my first day, we became instant best friends. After months of sharing bathrooms with our classmates and having awful roommates, we decided to rent a house off campus.

Luckily, between the money I had saved from working at my mom's florist shop through high school and Ash's current job at the nicest restaurant in Corvallis, we were set to rent our cute two-bedroom home right down the street from fraternity row.

That was where I met Ian.

I've only dated one person prior to him. But Ian is different; preppy and all about sports, he has a kindness towards me that drew me in. Plus, the fact that he hasn't complained too much about us not having sex yet is nice. I'm eighteen and I know it's a normal thing to do but I wanted to wait until I found the right guy. I think tonight is the night though. I mean, why wait any longer?

Ashley's voice brings me back to reality as she rambles on about a new guy she met the other night. But what about her current quest, Brian? I've never met the guy, but I thought things were going okay.

I nod, trying to listen as we pull into the driveway. I take a double take at the glossy black car parked next to mine on the left side of our narrow driveway; it must be a classic.

"Guess he got here early." Ashley shrugs, a small smile taking over her face.

"Are you two close? Why is he coming here?" I ask curiously.

"Aiden is his own thing. We're as close as he will let me be. You'll see what I'm talking about. He's coming here because he doesn't want to go home during his move."

His move?

"Why? I love your mom! She was so funny that time she came to visit and brought us both fuzzy pajamas and made us have a full-on girl's night, like a middle school throwback. Braided hair and all!" I laugh at the memory.

Ashley looks at me uneasily. "Look, don't say anything because it's a sore subject, but that's not his mom. He lives with our dad, sort of. If you can even call him one." Her lips twist into a frown. "But he's all Aiden has. He's been away the past four years at university and hasn't been back home since. He's looking for his own place, so he's staying here until then. Shouldn't be more than a couple of weeks." She shrugs.

"Your dad? The asshole that left you?" The astonishment is clear in my voice.

"Yeah, Aiden and I are half-siblings. I don't really want to get into that. Just please don't bring it up." She gives me a crooked grin as we step out of the car.

"Of course, I wouldn't." I smile reassuringly at her.

My thoughts go toward the little I know as Ashley doesn't talk much about her childhood. Her dad left her at a young age and isn't involved in her life. I just assumed they were full-blooded siblings.

Unlocking the door, I step inside. I whistle while walking to the kitchen, feeling ecstatic about my day. That's when I see him, leaning against the counter with his elbows on the bar top.

I can't help but stare, taking in the thin material of his T-shirt which showcases his inked and tan skin underneath. He looks up at me, his striking green eyes piercing mine. I feel my cheeks begin to heat but I can't pull my eyes away.

A cough interrupts my thoughts and I look over to find Ash looking back and forth between us. I assume they would hug after Aiden being gone for so long, but she simply waves.

"Hey Aiden," She greets with a smile.

"Hey Ash." His deep baritone fills our tiny kitchen. He straightens and makes his way over to her in long strides, ducking his head to miss the ceiling fan overhead. He is tall, so tall.

Muscles flex underneath his shirt, and when my eyes pan back to his face, he's already looking back at me. His full lips slightly curve upward, leaving the faintest trace of a smile.

I look away to keep from gawking. *What is wrong with me?* I shake my head to clear my mind.

Mine and Ashley's eyes simultaneously land on a tool bag, its contents laid out on the counter.

"What's this?"

A smirk creeps up on Aiden's face.

Dimples.

Then, as if something ruined his day, the smile is gone and replaced with a flat line.

He shrugs as he places everything back into the bag. "I used the key you left me to get inside. I went to wash my hands, but the hot water didn't work, so I fixed it."

Ashley's smile is evident, so is mine. The tap on our hot water has been broken since we moved in, but we've been too broke to fix it. Living off campus takes every dime we have, and while our house is cute… it needs some work.

We thank him numerous times until silence stretches through the small room. I can feel Aiden's sharp gaze traveling up and down my body.

Ashley speaks up then, gesturing my way.

"Anyway, this is Emma."

"Hello."

His voice is smooth like velvet, sending a chill through me. Maybe I'm worked up because I know what I'm doing tonight with Ian. That must be it. Hormones and all.

I awkwardly nod back at him, with a short smile. "Hey. I'll let you two catch up."

I turn on my heels to escape his piercing gaze and head for my bedroom. *Maybe I'm just being paranoid.* Back to the very important matter at hand; it's four and I'm exhausted from the finals today. With the party starting at ten, I can get some sleep in before we go. Plopping down on my bed, it takes slim minutes of my head resting on the pillow before I slide into a dreamless sleep.

"Em!" Ashley's slim hands wrap around my shoulders, gently shaking me from my slumber.

"I'm up, I'm up!" I mumble sleepily, sitting up to stretch my stiff body. Wiping the sleep from my eyes, I see we're not alone.

Leaning against the door frame is Aiden, who is looking at me with an unreadable expression. He glances at my body and I quickly cover up with the blanket, hiding that I'm in a tank top and boy shorts.

"Umm, let me get dressed." I say, looking past Ashley.

"Aiden! Get out!" She turns around and yells playfully at him, her feet stomping to the door and slamming it in his face.

He laughs deeply as he walks down the hall.

7

"I'm going to jump in the shower, then we can get ready!" I throw on some shorts and make my way down the hall towards the bathroom with some pep in my step.

I turn on the shower and run my fingers through the cool water as it warms, something I haven't felt in months. I can hear Ashley and Aiden talking in the living room, it's muffled but I catch a few things.

"I'm not going to a frat party." His tone is final.

I can imagine Ashley pouting right now.

"Fine! I just wanted to spend time with you." She huffs before I hear her stomping down the hallway.

Steam fills the small bathroom and I climb in, luxuriating in the warm water. Normally if we have time, we will go down to the frat house and use theirs but using our own is much better. I try and relax myself from my nerves about tonight as water cascades down my tan skin. I can't believe I'm going to do this, but I know Ian wants to, and I don't see why I should wait any longer.

I make sure to perfectly shave everywhere before I turn the water off. I reach towards the hook and swipe across an empty wall. Water drips on the floor as I step out to look under the sink. *Great, no towels.*

Opening the door slightly, I peek my head out, concealing my body behind the doorframe. "Ash!" I whisper-yell as I look down the hall for her.

"She's in her bathroom."

I jump back at the sound of Aiden's boots against the hardwoods as he gets closer to me. His fingers wrap around the edge of the door before he comes into full view. I feel my cheeks heat. I know he can't see me, but I am completely naked and dripping wet. His eyes burn into mine and I shyly look away.

"I need a towel," I say in an almost whisper.

"Why?" He crosses his tattooed arms across his broad chest, looking amused with himself.

"Umm, I'm naked!" I state the obvious, unsure why he has such a boyish grin. *Does he enjoy my embarrassment?*

"I see that. Well, I don't see much because of the doo..." His emerald eyes take in my red cheeks. In one smooth motion, he brushes a large hand through his thick black hair, pushing it up and out of his face. Of course, it sits perfectly where he wants it too.

I realize I'm staring, again.

"Aiden! What are you doing?!" Ashley's small feet patter down the hallway at a fast pace.

I sigh in relief when she comes to the door, her hair wrapped in a towel.

"What's wrong?" Her blue eyes take in my red cheeks.

"Towel." Is all I manage to say.

She nods and turns towards Aiden. "You, go." She demands.

He laughs, throwing his hands up innocently and walks away.

My savior returns moments later with a knock and I open the door slightly to grab the fluffy white towel. I meticulously go through my routine, moisturizer, lotion, brushing my unruly hair. Making sure the towel is wrapped tight, I swiftly make my way to my bedroom where Ashley is. Her hair dryer drowns out all sounds, her dirty blonde hair blowing with the hot heat.

"That was weird earlier, right?" Ashley rakes a brush through her hair, turning off the noisy dryer.

"What was weird?" I look at her innocently, not wanting to talk about the bathroom incident.

"You two gawking at each other in the kitchen. Then the bathroom thing," She comments nonchalantly.

I'm mortified my staring earlier was obvious. "Umm, yeah I just... I-"

She cuts me off. "Don't worry about it. I'm used to all of my friends having a crush on him." She waves her hand in front of her with a cheeky smile.

"I don't have a crush on him!" With red cheeks, I walk towards my closet and take off the towel, rustling the water out of my hair.

"Okay, whatever you say." She snickers.

I ignore her as I pick out what I'm wearing tonight. My eyes fixate on the yellow dress Ian mentions looks okay on me. I slip on the bright lacey dress, humming along to the music Ashley has on in the background.

The yellow looks good against my sun-kissed skin and boost my confidence. The neckline accentuates my cleavage in a good way, not too much but just enough. I make sure the matching new white lace bra and panties are neatly in order underneath my dress. I'm confident, well to a point, about tonight. I hope it's perfect and I hope there aren't too many people at the frat house.

"Why don't you just tell him you're coming?" Ashley fans mascara over her already long lashes.

"I want tonight to be special."

"Is that why you put on that matching bra and panties set?" She teases with a sly smile.

"Don't make me more nervous." I blush.

"Wait! You don't mean…oh my God, Em! You're going to sleep with him, aren't you?" She dramatically lays down on the floor.

"I think it's time." I shrug, unable to help the smile that creeps up my face.

"Come here! Sit down and let me do your make up!" She demands.

I sit in front of her with an awkward smile. I pull out my phone to see what he's up too as Ashley rummages through her bag, pulling out everything. I scroll to Ian's name and the butterflies dance in my stomach. I hope he isn't mad about me coming over unannounced.

Hey, babe! What are you up to?

I double check my make up in the mirror when I hear my text alarm sound and practically lunge for it.

Hey. Not much, just enjoying having a break from school now.

I don't know what to reply as I begin to question my decision to go. I mean I missed him, but I don't want to bug him if he's relaxing.

I'm sure he will be happy about tonight, I tell myself over and over in my head, *it's just sex.*

I stand to look in the full-length mirror when

Ashley announces she is done. I smooth my dress down and look at my face. She definitely pulled out all the stops, she even curled my hair with a large wand. She is so talented with make-up; I look much better than I did earlier.

My dark wavy hair cascades down my shoulders. My face looks sun-kissed, with faint freckles peeking out on my nose. The smokey black around my usual boring hazel eyes makes them look deeper and full of life. I blush at the sight of myself, but it's hidden under the rosy color Ashley put on my cheeks.

"Thank you." I grip the bottom of my yellow dress and sway back and forth like a giddy schoolgirl.

"Em, you look hot!" She makes me blush for what feels like the hundredth time today.

"Can we go? I'm nervous and I just want to get there." I throw on a pair of white wedges.

We make our way down the narrow hall, giggling. I almost forget we have a guest but it's hard to forget Aiden. I've learned in a short period of time that he takes all the attention in a room.

He lounges on the couch, a well-worn out book in his hands. He creases a corner and slowly closes it as he looks over at us. His gaze meets my eyes, then down my body. I turn to look towards Ashley, who is messing with her skirt. When I look back towards Aiden, I see his lips are slightly parted.

"Hey, Ash. Can I go to that party?" His tone is nicer, calmer than the discussion they had earlier.

She glares at him for a moment, considering his

request. Ignoring him, she says with sarcasm, "I thought you didn't want to go to a college party since you graduated all of five minutes ago and are too cool now." Her voice fades off as she disappears into the kitchen.

His eyes hungrily sweep up and down my frame before his gaze locks on mine.

"I changed my mind."

Two

I try to decipher his words, why does he want to come with us so suddenly? "It's at my boyfriend's house. You're more than welcome to come!" I announce sheepishly, pulling my eyes away from his smoldering gaze. I don't know why I'm so shaken by the way he stares so deeply at me, but it isn't right. Right?

"Sounds like fun." His smooth velvety voice washes over me.

I can't help but follow his fluid movements. His large hand lazily reaches over to grab the heavy black boots that are neatly placed at the edge of the couch. Ink swirls out from the bottom of his short sleeves, momentarily mesmerizing me.

Ashley peers around the kitchen and stares at her brother. "So, what happened to you not doing frat parties?"

A simple laugh escapes his lips. "I don't care for the entitled guys in a frat." He looks at me with such purpose I feel as if his words are directed at me, then his head swings back to Ash. "Do you want me to come or not?" He asks flatly, his jawline as sharp as a knife.

She perks up. "Yes, of course! Just change or something." She waves her hands at him.

He laughs before standing and heading for the door. "I'm good."

Grabbing his keys from the coffee table, I follow him. To be honest, he is. With his crisp white t-shirt and black jeans with matching black boots, he looks heavenly. *Oh my God, what is wrong with me?* I shake my head, struggling to keep up with his long strides.

"I'm driving."

We pile into the leather seats of Aiden's classic black car. My eyes pan around the spacious interior, I'm curious what the make is. Trying to not be obvious, I tilt my head to the side as I attempt to find an emblem somewhere.

"It's a Challenger." He says, his eyes trained on me. I don't miss the way the golden interior light makes his green eyes shimmer, something that looks out of character for his so far serious demeanor, I simply ignore it instead.

I nod with a smile, noticing for the first time that I had jumped in the front without thinking. Ashley may have wanted to sit with her brother. I think about saying something, but when I look over at Aiden, he flashes me a brilliant smile as he rests his hand across the back of the seat. Ashley stays quiet as she fiddles with her phone. I guess she didn't give it a second thought.

The engine roars to life as Aiden turns the key in the ignition and we make the short three-minute drive. My tiny hope that the party will be small is gone, as I see the front yard riddled with drunk people celebrating summer break. My slightly shaking hand reaches for the door handle as we come to a stop.

Heads turn in our direction as the engine shuts off, making it momentarily quiet. A few girls begin whispering as they take in Aiden. I don't blame them. He is something wonderful to look at. I take one last glance before shaking the thoughts from my head. I never look at other guys this way.

Stepping into the warm summer air, I note the sweet scent of honeysuckles. Inhaling deeply, I try to place this moment somewhere in my mind to keep it safe. I've been waiting for this night since forever. My strides are confident as I walk ahead of Ashley and Aiden, stepping through the threshold and into the frat house. I almost sink into the floor at the sight of the crowd.

"Hey, Em!" A familiar voice calls from the living room.

"Hey, Becca!" I greet in excitement, heading towards the couch where a few people I know are seated.

Becca has always been so sweet when I visit. I'm grateful that Ian's friends are always so welcoming. She sits with her legs propped against her boyfriend, Alec, as he twirls her long crimson red lock between his fingers. She always reminds me of Ariel from The Little Mermaid.

"Long time no see." Becca sticks her bottom lip out.

Giving a nervous smile, I try to hold a conversation even though my nerves are at an all-time high. "I know. I didn't want to intrude." I shrug. It isn't really my scene.

She laughs at my formality.

I tap my fingers against my bare knees, feeling out of my element. It's how I always feel when I come here. "Where's Ian at anyway?"

She answers by gesturing towards the stairs.

I nod, not wanting to get up just yet. Someone hands me a drink and I gulp it down. I have all the time in the world to go upstairs, I just need a few more minutes to relax.

I set the empty plastic cup down on the coffee table and look around, trying to find where the liquor is. My eyes trail to Ashley who is animated and deep in conversation with one of our classmates.

"Here." A velvet voice sparks to my right. Aiden gestures for me to take a red cup from his hand.

A smile forms on my lips. He doesn't know how much I need this. *But why is he bringing me one?*

"Thank you?"

He nods once, leaning down near my ear so I can hear him over the blaring music. "I know you come here often. But don't take drinks from anyone you don't know."

His warm breath caresses my exposed neck, sending an unfamiliar shiver down my spine. I really need to go see Ian and rid my mind of my hormones.

I laugh lightly. He has a point but still... "I'm accepting a drink from you, and I don't know you."

His eyes narrow slightly, as though commanding me to stare into his sharp features, not seeing my humor. "Just–" He cuts himself off with a shake of his head. "Where is your boyfriend?" His tone has a hint of accusation.

"Upstairs," I say nervously, questioning myself. *What if he isn't happy to see me?*

Aiden straightens, his height is intimidating. Crossing his arms, he surveys me. "Maybe he's sleeping? We could go?" He offers, but I don't know why.

The idea of him sleeping during a party makes me laugh. I shake my head. "I'm going to go find him in a minute."

Deep in thought, he bites his lip. Then, as if a switch has been flipped, he shakes his head once while directing his attention back to the other side of the room. A crooked smile plays on his face. I follow his line of sight to where a girl stands. With her eyes trained on him, she gives a small wave at his acknowledgment.

"I'll be over there with Ash. Just don't accept drinks from strangers." He deadpans, walking away from me without another glance.

In a slow calculated movement, he stands before the girl. She giggles when he talks to her. Of course, he's the type of guy to hook up with random girls at a party where he knows absolutely no one. I look back to Ian's friends and ignore the odd feeling in my chest.

My nerves settle as I get lost in conversation, enjoying a few more drinks that I make myself in the kitchen.

Deciding it's time, I stand up and smooth my dress down.

I wanted Ian to randomly find me, maybe come downstairs and get the hint of my surprise visit, so I don't have to make the first move. But screw it, I feel strong and confident. I'm ready to find him myself.

I turn towards the staircase, watching Aiden follow my movements with alert eyes while propped against the wall. The striking girl from before is still demanding his attention, which is now on me. His narrowed eyes never leave me as he lifts a beer bottle to his full lips and takes a smooth sip.

Averting my gaze, which seems to keep wandering in his direction, I rush up the stairs, my feet hitting the boards in sync with the thumping music. Anticipation and puzzlement fill me as I turn the knob to Ian's room.

Why is his door closed? Maybe he is asleep?

I throw the door open and my breath hitches at the sight before me. The chaotic noise from downstairs fades away as I discover sounds of nightmares I never knew existed. A drowning pain soaks into my chest.

I urge my legs to move as I watch him thrust into her naked body, but they remain rooted to the ground. He hovers over her, his hips pumping, eliciting hideous moans from her so loud that it masks the tiny whimper that slips past my lips.

As I watch him kiss her, my legs buckle, and I collapse to the floor with a thud. Yet, the pain is nothing compared to the shattering of my heart.

His head snaps back. "Get the fuck ou–" He cuts himself off when he sees me and pushes the girl away. Wrapping a sheet around his waist, he reaches for me.

Unable to stand being in his room for another second, the images from earlier now burnt into my mind, I bolt. Bursting through the front door, I inhale deeply.

Stupid honeysuckles.

The lawn is still riddled with drunken people but in my frantic state, they part as I shove them away.

I need to get out of here, to get away.

"Emma!"

Anger courses through my veins at the sound of his voice, still thick with lust. I shake in disgust as I turn to face Ian, my arms crossed. He has a pair of basketball shorts on but is shirtless still.

I hold a finger up. If eyes could kill, he'd be dead.

"No! Don't ever talk to me again. I was coming over tonight to..." I shake my head with a scoff. "Oh my god. This is fucked, Ian." I scream, running my hands through my hair and destroying my perfectly placed curls.

A crowd has gathered around us, but I don't care. I only see red and the longer he looks at me with a confused expression the deeper the shade of red grows.

"You were coming for wha–"

I cut him off with a slash of my hand.

Ian stands before me within a few strides. He smells like her and pungent alcohol. I stamp down the sudden wave of nausea. The emotions coursing through me are overwhelming.

"I have been nothing but good to you! But then I come here tonight to find you in bed with some skank?" I bellow out my desperation and betrayal.

In one quick movement, I slap him across the face. The sharp crack echoes in the now quiet night. A wave of satisfaction washes over me when I see the red bloom on his skin. I want him to feel a fraction of the humiliation I feel. Plus, I know how much he hates it when he's embarrassed.

With one menacing step, he closes the gap between us. I move to take a step back, but his large hands grip my shoulder tightly, a dark look forms in his eyes. I've never seen this side of Ian before. I try to squirm out of his grip, but I'm stuck.

"How dare you embarrass me in front of all these people." Ian spits out.

My head lowers slightly, momentarily regretting my hasty act. But when I close my eyes, all I see is him on top of her, their moans echoing in my ears. Rage rushes through me and I lift my hand subconsciously.

With a growl, Ian grabs my wrist so hard a gasp escapes my lips.

"Don't even fucking think about it." A deep voice demands from behind me, and I begin to worry I pissed off one of his stupid frat brothers.

"Fuck off, dude. This is none of your business." Ian glares down, or should I say up, at the speaker.

An odd sense of relief fills me as I turn to see Aiden quickly making his way over.

"Take your hands off her," Aiden growls darkly as he steps next to me.

A deep chuckle escapes Ian's lips.

I frown. I think I've pushed him to his breaking point.

"Fuck it. She can't be that mad. I've been trying to fuck her for the past three months and she just won't give it up." Ian admits.

I gasp as he forcefully throws my wrist down, releasing me.

"What? But you…" I choke back my tears. *What is he talking about?*

Aiden steps between us, gently nudging my body back. He leans towards me and coaxes in a soft voice, "Go, Emma. Be a good girl. Get in my car," before slipping the keys in my trembling hands.

Unmoving and in shock, I simply stare at his car, tears brimming in my eyes.

Ian lets out a careless, drunken laugh. "I didn't know you were coming tonight. This really isn't my fault."

I shake my head. I don't know who this stranger is. He's oozing typical frat boy behavior, something he claimed to detest.

Aiden sighs and turns his attention towards Ian, pinning him with dark eyes. "I warned you just now. Leave her alone."

I take comfort in the deep growl of his voice towards my boyfriend. *No, my ex.*

"Why did you give her your keys? Who are you?" Ian's eyes narrow in anger.

A smirk plays on Aiden's face, his tone oozing boredom towards Ian. "I don't see why that's any of your business." Aiden's presence alone should make someone like Ian back down immediately, but he's drunk and not thinking things through.

Ian takes note of the crowd; his frat brothers, and the girls I thought were my friends are staring in shock. After what happened, I am still surprised by Ian's cocky demeanor.

"Honestly, I don't care." He laughs. "Maybe she'll give it up to you. Good luck with tha–"

Aiden's knuckles connect with Ian's jaw, cutting him off.

I watch in awe as Ian lands flat on the ground, his eyes slightly open, and turns to spit out blood. He smirks arrogantly up at Aiden and I realize it's a stupid decision, as Aiden violently jumps on top of him and begins to bash his face into the damp grass. His muscles flex with every rapid movement, threatening to rip his fitted white T-shirt.

"Aiden, please stop. Please!" I plead through muffled sobs.

A deep rage swirls in his green eyes when Aiden looks back at me.

I stare in horror at the sight of Ian. Unable to help myself, despite all the awful things he did, I kneel beside him and examine his wounds.

Aiden stares at me in disbelief. "You can't be fucking serious!" He exclaims through ragged breaths. I see him move to walk away but hesitate.

Ian winces as I prod his face. He glares at me with so much anger, before pushing me off him and onto the grass. "Get off me, you stupid bitch."

Aiden's long legs glide back to us.

Instinctively, I throw myself over Ian to protect him.

Why did I do that? I don't know. Pretty much the entire house is outside, and I probably look like an idiot. But there must be a reason for this. The alcohol is muddling my ability to think.

I stare down at his face, seeing nothing behind his blank blue eyes.

"Nope, fuck this. You're not doing this," Aiden mutters into my ear.

In one swift movement, I'm no longer on the ground but slung over Aiden's shoulder as he heads towards his car. I can feel his arm securely below my butt, preventing any accidents from happening. Oddly, it warms my heart. I kick a little, but I'm suddenly exhausted.

"I'll let you down once you calm down, but I'm not allowing you to embarrass yourself. Did you even hear what he just said to you?" His tone is laced with disgust.

"I do, I do remember. But I love him, and he lo–"

"You're too sweet for your own good." Aiden sighs. "I don't know what you see in him. I only met him for two minutes and I already despise the guy."

"You don't even know me!" I scoff, hitting his back.

He opens the passenger door and carefully deposits me in the seat. He reaches around and buckles me in while I put my hands over my face in embarrassment of everything that has just happened.

I see Ashley rushing through the chaotic scene towards us through my fingers.

"Get in and don't talk about it." He orders, gesturing towards his side of the car.

Ash simply nods and climbs in the back from the driver's seat. She peeks around my seat, her emotions raw, and rubs my shoulder in console.

Aiden glances towards Ian who is now standing, breathing heavily, as he glares in our direction. His fist is balled but he doesn't dare to come closer.

Worried, I reach out the open window and grab Aiden's shaking arm. His eyes meet mine and I watch as the rage tries to calm. There's an internal struggle behind his eyes, but I see the resolve when his face finally softens.

Aiden shakes his head once, coming around to the driver side.

Then he yells menacingly, pointing his finger accusingly at Ian. "Fuck you."

I'm thankful when he cranks the car up and the engine drowns out the scene we are driving away from and my sobs.

My thoughts run through my head as though they're trying to win a race. So lost in thought, I haven't realized we are in the driveway.

It's pitch black outside. Aiden flips on the interior light, the color is a warm tone. I'm thankful it's subtle, and it doesn't worsen my headache. He opens my door and kneels, staring at me with a worried expression.

My head tilts to the empty backseat. "Where is she?" My small voice is sore from my screaming earlier.

"I told her to go inside." Aiden brings his large hand to rest on my knee in a comforting notion.

The warm touch is nice; it makes me feel less alone in the wide cab of his car. His large hand splayed out on my knee looks almost sinful. I can feel his rough callouses brushing against my soft skin as he trails his palms in circular motions in a comforting manner.

The hands of a man, something I've never experienced. Adjusting to the warm light I notice for the first time that his knuckles are busted, bleeding from his altercation with Ian.

"Your hands! Are you okay?" I bite my bottom lip with concern, guilty he got hurt because of me.

He looks down and a smile creeps up his face. "Don't worry about that. Were you two together long?" His tone is light.

I ponder the question. It isn't about the time we were together. I'm more upset that I believed he cared for me when he obviously didn't.

"We weren't together long at all. Maybe three months between us meeting to dating and now...this." I gesture to my tear-soaked face, mascara undoubtedly falling on my cheeks.

"He doesn't deserve you." He states, concern thick in his voice.

The sentiment causes a light smile to spread on my lips, but the overwhelming embarrassment crashes down overhead. "I can't believe he said those things to me. Everyone must think I'm so naive. I really thought he liked me for me, like really liked me."

Saying it out loud makes me feel worse about myself. *How blind am I?*

"First off, being naive isn't a bad thing, as long as you have people around you who won't take advantage of you. I think your trust is just in the wrong people." His thumb gently rolls circles on my leg, trying to console me.

Between his warm and calming tone, and his soothing touch, I calm. "I should have known better, really." I shake my head. "He is a star Lacrosse player and a senior, and I'm this." I gesture to myself, feeling less confident than I did when I left.

"No man would want to wait to have sex

27

anyway," I remark absentmindedly.

"He is not a *man*." A sound emanates deep in his broad chest, as his deep jade eyes pierce me.

He quickly composes himself. "No man would have spoken to you that way, or pushed you off of him. Those things should be saved for the bedroom, with a real man, when you want those things to be done to you, for fun."

My cheeks burn with the intensity of his stare and the seductiveness of his words. "I'm just glad I didn't give him my virgi—"

I cut myself off. He may be Ashley's brother, but I don't really know him. I'm not sure why I'm so comfortable around him. Maybe it's because of his concern and how closely he's listening to me.

"I'm sorry. I need to go," I rush out as I go to grab the handle.

"Absolutely not." He commands. I sit back against the leather seat, taken back by the change in mood. "It's his loss. I'm happy he didn't. You saved yourself from that whole situation. Besides, you shouldn't have to sleep with someone just to get them to stay with you." I stare at him with mild shock at his frankness.

"Thank you?" *This is embarrassing.*

"You needed to hear it. You ready to go in now?"

I nod as I slide out of his car and he follows me in.

"Can I help you?" I ask, heading towards the first aid kit. He looks at me inquisitively as if he doesn't understand my question. I point to his bloodied knuckles,

28

"I'll clean and bandage them."

His head tilts slightly, examining me. "No, you need your rest. I'll be fine." Another hint of a smile flashes on his face, is he not used to someone helping him?

I grant myself one last glance as I walk towards my room.

Aiden plops down on the couch and grabs the worn-out book from the coffee table. His feet dangle off the edge about a foot. Our couch is way too small for his massive frame, it makes me laugh a little.

I lay down in bed and wait for the tears to come, but they have all been used up. I laugh at myself, to think I even cried over that asshole. It's the shock of the events that upset me, the way Ian spoke to me. I'm an idiot for even considering sleeping with him. How juvenile of me to get so upset over a guy I have only known for three months.

I'm happy that Aiden had hit him. I don't like violence, but it felt nice to have someone stick up for me. A man to take charge of a situation that upset me, he seems like a gentleman. A sense of calm washes over me as I wrap the blankets tighter around me and I slip into a dreamless sleep.

Three

A iden's first week with us passes by in a confusing blur.

  I spend the better of the week in bed, drowning myself in sappy heartbreak movies and tissue boxes. I keep away from Aiden, wanting to confide in him more, but not wanting to bother him. I can't shake the way his green eyes drink me in when I stumbled sleepily into the kitchen the next morning. Or maybe it's a hallucination created by my insecurity to make me feel better about being cheated on.

  I learn a few things about this otherwise mysterious man over the course of a week.

  He enjoys his coffee black, two cups every morning. He reads while watching the news; how he does it, I do not know. It takes complete silence for me to get lost in the pages. When he concentrates, his brows furrow and his edges harden. I don't think I've seen a more defined jawline in my life.

My unexplainable interest in him bothers me.

Why do I care so much? Why does his presence affect me so thoroughly?

I barely know him, yet I can't resist the magnetic pull I feel whenever he walks into a room, towering over everyone and demanding attention with one breath. But I just got out of a relationship, bouncing from one man to the next isn't me.

Still, I can't deny this one-sided attraction.

Maybe it was the way he spoke to me when I was at my lowest. That must be it. He made me feel better during such a humiliating time and I'm just feeling grateful. I'm humoring myself anyways. Someone like him will never be interested in someone like me, a schoolgirl drooling over her best friend's much older, and very successful brother.

"Em."

The gentle sound of Ashley's voice wakes me. I rustle in my blankets and peek up, seeing her next to the bed, cradling a box of chocolates.

A smile instantly creeps on my face. She's given me so much space since that night. School was over, and I had nowhere to be. She knew I needed to relax in solitude, and she granted me that.

"Ash." My voice is thick from sleeping so much. She sits down beside me on the bed.

"I know we haven't talked much. I'm so sorry

about last weekend. I didn't know your brother would fight him. I ruined your first night of seeing him in so long." Guilt laces my voice.

"Are you kidding me? I spent the last five days with him while you were in here. I'm already sick of him," She jokes, her smile sympathetic. "First off, Aiden fights...everyone."

I try to imagine it. He definitely has the build for it, and he takes obvious care of his body by the glances I caught of him with his shirt off after he came inside from a long run.

And I remember the rage in his eyes that night. But to me, he is gentle. I feel a little less special about Aiden saving me now that I know him fighting is a regular thing and not because of the way Ian treated me.

"Oh." Is all I manage to say.

"You okay?" Ashley twirls a lock of my brown hair around her finger, concern plastered on her face.

"I know I've been sulking, but I do feel better. Where did you go that night when we got home by the way? I was going to talk to you but ended up talking to Aiden," I question quietly.

"Yeah, I was really surprised when he practically kicked me out of the car once we pulled in the driveway. I've never seen him be so nice to someone before. He normally doesn't care about anything." She laughs, but her eyes pan downward in confusion.

"I thought you said he fights a lot?" I'm confused. "Obviously he likes confrontation."

Ashley shakes her head. "He does, but it's

different. He talked to you. You were in the car for half an hour. The confrontation happened with Ian. But with you, he looked concerned. It's just normally not his thing." She shrugs, looking at me with curious eyes. "He filled me in on what Ian said, so I'm assuming that's what got him heated. I still can't believe he did that to you!" She balls up her small fist as her face scrunches in anger.

"Honestly, I don't want to talk about Ian anymore. I can't believe I thought he loved me. How stupid. We barely know each other." I lament in an exhausted voice.

"It's normal to be upset. Yes, you weren't together long, but you were comfortable enough around him to think about...you know." She sighs.

The silence draws out for several long seconds before Ashley jumps up with a smile. "Let's dress up and go out tonight!"

"I don't know, Ash." I throw the comforter off me. The idea of fun does sound good though.

"Please," She pleads through batted lashes.

"Fine." With a sigh, I cave.

"I'm coming too." Aiden calls down the hall in a serious tone.

We burst out into laughter.

I wonder how much of that conversation he heard.

"Protective older brother much?"

"It isn't me he wants to protect." Ashley whispers with a sly smile.

Aiden is in Portland, an hour and a half drive away.

I'm guessing he's looking for apartments there. I wonder what he does, what his major was. He exudes confidence and wealth when you look at him, I just have no idea what his career path could be.

My curiosity on a high, I search our small house for Ashley. I find her on the couch with her laptop open, typing violently against the keyboard.

"Ash? You okay?" I assess her behavior, her fingers meticulously and harshly combing the keyboard with a little more force than necessary.

She clicks one more button before slamming her laptop shut. Turning to me, she slaps a manufactured smile on her face. "Yeah, I was just sending my English teacher a few choice words on an e-mail for giving me a seventy on my final. It was an essay about 'love', which is supposed to be subjective!"

"Miss. Parks?" I ask with a laugh.

She makes an air check mark and huffs. "Yup, that's the one."

"I think you'll be okay. You have a what...ninety-seven in that class?" I stifle a laugh.

She groans. "I wanted a perfect one hundred. That essay is thirty percent of our grade! She's just angry her husband left her last year. I mean, why make us write that for a final if you're scorned and don't want to hear about love?" She places the laptop on the table beside the book Aiden was reading yesterday.

I take a seat on the couch, smiling in surprise

when I see the title.

"Aiden reads classic novels?" I eye the bent and tattered copy of The Merchant of Venice.

"Yeah, it's weird right?" She laughs while gesturing to the book. "He's always been a reader. When he came to visit when I was younger, he would read instead of playing with the neighborhood kids. I always wondered why he went down the corporate road, you would have thought he'd be a writer with the amount of time he spends with his face buried in a book."

"Corporate? Aiden?" I ask, astounded.

"I know. With the tattoos, it seems odd, right?" She pulls her thick hair through a scrunchie and leans back on our couch. "He went to Stanford and got his bachelor's in finance," She announces proudly.

I nearly choke on air before I compose myself. "Wow, that's amazing! Does your dad have money like that?"

I know Ashley is on a scholarship, as her mom doesn't have a ton of money. She has no contact with her dad, but it seems like Aiden does. I remember her saying she originally wanted to go south for school. I'm glad she decided against it or we would have never crossed paths.

She lets out a loud laugh. "No way. Even if he did, there's no way Aiden would want shit from him. Aiden is completely self-made. He got a full ride for his academics in high school." She beams.

I understand why she's proud. That's a huge accomplishment at twenty-five. I ponder this for a second; a full ride to Stanford. He must be insanely smart.

I try to tamper down my attraction and nerves, knowing he has brains to go with his brawns. Could he be any more perfect?

"He told me about how his classmates glared at him for a few weeks when he started." She laughs, waving her hand absentmindedly. "I mean a guy who looks like Aiden, covered in tattoos, has to be quite the unusual student at a school like that. But his brilliance showed through, and the students there quickly realized it I'm guessing. He made some really great friends there. I know he was sad to graduate but he's ready to start his life in Portland."

It's scary how Ashley can read my thoughts.

"Why Portland?" I rest my elbows on my knees, listening intently.

"That's what he's doing today. He intern-ed before college, making investments for high up businessmen. He's so good at what he does, he made his own investments early. He owns some properties there, which is why he wants to move there."

"He's also leasing a floor of a high rise, so he has somewhere to meet with his bigger investors. Some of them can be... intimidating." She looks at me uneasily. "Others are your normal run of the mill rich men. He's going to check out his new office and see about his lease on the apartment. That's why he's staying here for a while, so they can get it finished." She concludes with another proud smile.

I straighten. "What do you mean by intimidating?"

"I don't know how to explain it. Almost like the Mafia is what I would guess. Aiden can handle himself, so he takes those clients when no one else will. I don't know much about it, but I would stay away from his work if I were you." She laughs humorlessly.

"What does he do though, like his title?"

"He's a private investor. I'm not really sure what it entails. You have to remember we don't talk all that much. But from what I know, he's great with numbers. I believe he purchases investments for CEOs and things like that?" She questions herself.

"Good for him! That's awesome, he's already got a job that quick. I hope when I graduate, I can find somewhere I fit in." I hide my internal frown with an outward smile. Everyone has their lives figured out.

My current major is the opposite of what I want to do. My dream is to become a pastry chef. I would love to be able to go to a culinary school. While OSU offers a wonderful culinary program, I have to be realistic about it. My mom works so hard to pay for my schooling. I don't want to graduate and have nowhere to go career wise. I'm taking the safe route in life, but what else could I do?

Ashley's words surprise me.

"He didn't get a job, he owns the company." She smiles. "Don't stress. He's older than us. We're only freshman, you have plenty of time to plan your life." She reassures.

"Why did he just graduate if he's twenty-five?"

"Well, after high school, he took a three-year

internship before starting at Stanford. That's how he got his money and started his business."

I raise my brow. "Did he always know he wanted to do this?"

"You're curious about him, aren't you?" She examines me shrewdly.

"No. no. I mean, maybe?"

She throws her hands up. "Look, truly, if you want to go after him, I don't care. It's not like we are in high school, you're both adults."

A laugh escapes my lips. "Yeah, I don't think that'll be a problem. He's nice to me, but I don't think he is interested." I dismiss her thoughts. "Plus, the whole Ian thing." I shudder from the humiliation I received at his hand.

"Oh, fuck Ian," She bellows. "As for Aiden, I wouldn't be so sure that he's not interested."

I blush. "I mean, he's just a nice guy."

She scoffs. "To you, he is. You barely left your room all week. I had to tell him multiple times not to bother you. He's been asking about you non-stop. Every other friend of mine that he's met, he has ignored with obvious annoyance." She smiles teasingly. "Plus, you need someone to take your mind off of that preppy douchebag."

Armed with a pillow, I let out a war-cry and hit her with it. A fight quickly ensues as Ashley grabs two throws from the couch and hurls them at me. Laughter booms throughout the living room and soon, we crumble in a fit of giggles onto the couch. My legs are thrown up over the back of the couch while my back rests on the bottom cushions.

A deep cough interrupts our childish fight and we snap towards the sound.

My jaw involuntarily drops as I take in the sight of Aiden leaning against the door frame. His black hair is slicked back perfectly. His emerald eyes look deeper than usual. He exudes a serious vibe, which matches his attire. A black suit with a black dress shirt underneath. His tattoos are barely visible, but I see one peeking through as he undoes his cuffs.

I force my jaw shut and swallow hard. My eyes travel to his face, where his eyes burn into mine. That's when I realize I'm just in my panties and a tank top. I flip my body around quickly and search for a blanket. I grab the one Aiden used the night before and cover myself, trying to ignore the delicious scent it's laced with. Subconsciously, I take a deep breath. *Leather and mint.*

"Hey girls." He greets in a stern tone, but his teasing smile creeps up, softening his rough edges.

"You look all business, Aiden," Ashley teases.

He rolls his eyes and saunters down the hallway. "I'm going to get changed."

"Stop gawking." She nudges me.

Fearing Aiden heard her attempted whisper, I peek up just as he turns the bathroom doorknob. My stomach drops as his face turns slightly. The sexiest half smile graces his perfect features, and my face burns from embarrassment.

I hit Ashley once more with the pillow after he

disappears into the bathroom.

Once the water starts running, I glare at her with burning cheeks. "He heard you!" I quietly scream at her.

She shrugs and we fall into a fit of laughter.

I scuttle to my room and throw on some jeans. I need to get the sight of him in that suit out of my head, quickly. "I'm going to run some errands," I call out as I grab the necessities before running out. *It's a nice day. A drive through town is just what I need.*

After a few hours, my backseat is full of essentials we need for the summer as I head for the mall.

Maybe a new dress is what I need to rebuild my confidence.

I'm met with way too many options, but a black mini dress catches my eye. I grab my size and go into the dressing room. I squeeze into the tight-fitting dress and turn to look at myself.

A smile appears on my face. *I love it!*

I usually go for something a little less revealing, but I need a change. It hugs my curves perfectly and I feel...sexy. I giggle as I run my hands over the soft fabric. The neckline is low, so I won't be able to wear a bra, and the back is cut low. There isn't much material, but I feel surprisingly comfortable.

The sun has set when I pull into the empty driveway.

Aiden probably made plans and isn't joining us

tonight. I sigh as I step out of my car and throw the heavy bags over my arms before heading in. *I'm not making a second trip.*

Setting the bags down in the foyer, I head for the kitchen to look for something to eat, only to find a note on the counter.

Hey! We ran to get pizza. Hurry and get dressed! We are leaving at 10. Love you, xoxo Ash

I glance at the clock and see that it's nine. *Where did the time go?*

Running to the foyer, I grab my dress and rush to my room to get ready. I start with my make-up, spending more time than usual on my eyes, focusing on making them a little darker than normal. Surprisingly, I finish fairly quickly and begin to curl my hair.

I hear the door open and feet shuffling.

"Hey!" I yell as I twist the last lock around the large wand.

Ashley enters with a box of pizza and sits on the hardwood floor. Her hair and makeup are perfect but she's in jeans and a t-shirt. Just as I begin to worry about my dress, she smiles and hands me a slice. I place the wand down on the marble slab where it normally sits, before digging in.

"I'll throw on my dress later. I'm wearing the red one. What do you think?"

I sigh in relief, not wanting to look overdressed. "I love that one!"

It isn't long before Ashley stands up. "I'm going to change. Be ready in ten minutes!" She says excitedly as she bounces out of the room.

Following her lead, I shut the door and climb into my new black dress. I slide on a tall pair of black heels with a thin ankle strap and take one last look in the full-length mirror. The dress looks even better with my hair and makeup done.

Excited to show Ashley my new outfit, maybe Aiden too, I smile as I leave my room. A large hand wraps around my arm just as I pass the bathroom, making me jump.

Aiden's head dramatically sweeps in my direction, showcasing his diamond sharp jawline. "You're going out in that?" his voice booms down the narrow hallway, his hand firmly yet gently holding me in place.

"Umm, is it bad?" I frown as I look down at my dress, questioning my chosen attire.

He drops my arm with a sigh. "Exact opposite," He states flatly. "Do you know how many guys I'm going to have to fight off tonight? They're going to be staring at you."

His seriousness makes me giggle. *I guess this is his way of giving compliments.* "I highly doubt you'll have that problem, Aiden."

I sense irritation in his green eyes. *Why does he care if guys stare at me? I'm just his sisters' best friend.*

His eyes travel languidly down my body. I watch as he pulls his bottom lip between his teeth, shuddering at the unexpected tingle of arousal that I feel. Abruptly, he walks away, leaving me breathless. "You look gorgeous, Emma," he comments just as he turns the corner.

Ashley admires my outfit with an appreciative gaze. "Em! That dress is amazing! You *have* to let me borrow it when I go out of town in a couple days!" She begs, feeling the material between her manicured nails.

I have forgotten she's visiting her on-again-off-again boyfriend for a few days. I wonder if Aiden will stay while she's gone.

"Thanks! And of course you can take it with you," I assure her.

We quickly head out to Aiden's car, where I slide into the front seat, again, without thinking. I glance at him, taking in how good he looks in such a simple outfit – dark jeans and a black T-shirt. His hair is messy, yet it looks perfect on him.

"Ash, where are we going?" He glances back in the rearview.

"The Lounge. It's not far. Just make a left turn out of the driveway and go about five miles. You can't miss it!" She squeals with excitement.

"You got the fakes?"

Ashley hands me mine; it looks enough like me to pass. We've been going to The Lounge for months. But the last time we were there, the new bartender turned us away, so we found a guy on campus who makes them so we wouldn't be turned away again.

Aiden eyes me. "Am I going to have to deal with the both of you being smashed?" He laughs but I sense sincerity in his teasing words.

We arrive at the familiar club, flashing lights beam through the barely tinted windows. I can hear the faint music coming from inside. It takes a minute to find a spot a distance away to park as the place is absolutely packed.

"Let's go!" Ash exclaims once we hop out of the car, and marches towards the club.

I try to keep up with her exuberant pace, slightly pacing Aiden and his long strides. Gently, I feel his hand slide to the small of my back, slowing me down. I match his movements as he walks by my side, curious as to why he wants to walk with me instead of letting me go ahead with Ash.

Aiden opens the door for me while Ash runs into the dimly lit club. I walk behind her, slowly assessing the mass amount of people staring at us, or I should say at Aiden. Girls gawk when he walks past, and I push myself a little closer against his side. Peeking over to gauge his reaction, I note a boyish grin on his face that causes a flutter in my stomach. I'm not sure why I'm being so protective over Ashley's brother, but he intrigues me.

Ash grabs my hand, yanking me away. With a shrug in Aiden's direction, we head for the bar.

"Three shots, please." Ashley yells over the thumping music and winks at the bartender.

Aiden clears his throat behind us. "Ash, I'm driving. I'm good. You girls have fun." Reaching into his dark jeans, he pulls out a wad of cash from a clip and places it in her hands.

Eyeing his kind gesture, I shake my head. "I can pay for mine, thank you though," I grin shyly as I move a little closer to him.

He chuckles, brushing his hand against my arm. "Don't worry about it. I came out tonight because I want the both of you to have fun without having to worry about your safety." He shrugs.

Ashley mouths thank you and he nods.

I grudgingly accept, not wanting to be rude. I guess it's something he normally does. Besides the twenty dollars of running money in my account doesn't really need to be spent on drinks. Yes, I know…I just bought a new dress, but I needed to do something for my confidence. I had more saved, but Ian needed some money and I idiotically gave it to him. I roll my eyes at myself.

Ashley hands me a clear shot of what I guess is vodka.

I down it quickly, wanting to forget about Ian and all the things I thought he was. My face scrunches at the taste; I will never get used to the uncomfortable burn straight liquor gives.

"Two more!" Ashley announces excitedly and we down another set.

"Slow down," Aiden whispers lowly in my ear, his minty breath tingling against my skin.

I nod. He's right. I'm not the best drinker and I don't want to get sick tonight. With a sigh, I lean back slightly against Aiden's body, relishing in how his hand easily comes up to rest on the small of my back.

There is something oddly comforting about the swirl of his thumb, and I push away all thoughts of how I shouldn't be feeling such things to make room for the butterflies that twirl inside my stomach.

Ash and I reminisce about our first year of college, celebrating our highs and lows. I'm in a low spot, but with her by my side, I'm already feeling much better.

Slipping money to the bartender without Aiden's watchful eye noticing is hard, but I succeed and order myself a Mai Tai to keep the good vibes flowing. I slowly stir my straw around the orange and pink liquid before bringing it to my lips. It's sweet and delicious, but strong. A small moan escapes my lips as sweet orange hits my throat, soothing the burning from the vodka earlier.

I tip my head up and see Aiden gently biting his bottom lip while staring at my lips. I quickly turn to Ashley, hiding my embarrassment.

"Let's dance!" I shout spontaneously with a bright smile, but turning to Aiden shyly. "Wanna come?"

He shakes his head with a crooked smile.

Ignoring his mesmerizing dimples, I grab Ashley's arm and drag her to the crowded dance floor.

Immediately, we begin swaying to the music. Each time I glance over at the bar, Aiden is watching me with narrowed eyes.

I lose myself in the music as time passes. My previously consumed alcohol hits me, hard, and I enjoy my brain being carefree. My body relaxes as the music flows through me.

"I love this song!" I say to Ash, only to realize she's nowhere to be found.

I scan the mass of thrumming bodies and find her dancing with a cute guy. She looks happy and I don't want to ruin her moment, even though she has Brian. They are so on and off that I never know when they're together. I think of Ian and the false security I felt in our relationship, and sadness washes over me.

I plod off the dance floor and scan the bar for Aiden, but I don't see him. I frown. Stumbling through the makeshift electronic mosh pit of people, I finally come across a small clearing ahead. A pair of hands suddenly grab my waist, making me stumble.

Aiden?

Turning my head, I frown at the stranger in front of me.

He's handsome, blonde and lean. Free of tattoos and endless emerald stares, my mind adds on. Aiden is so out of my reach yet I'm not sure why he's so embedded in my mind. Taking my time to observe the man, I admire his clean cut. He's wearing a pressed blue polo, his eyes a matching bright blue.

"Hey, beautiful," He murmurs into my ear.

I hit myself mentally when a bubble of giggles escapes when his breath tickles my neck.

"Hi," I mutter.

"Wanna dance?"

I nod absentmindedly. I wonder why I even bothered. He's already begun moving my hips with his hands. *Would Aiden care? But then again, why would he?*

I laugh at the thought of Aiden being interested in me. Shoving all thoughts away, I sway to the music as the bass rumbles through me.

Aiden

I had to take a lap around the club, with how mad Emma's dancing is driving me.

I don't know why I'm so interested in the girl. She's young, but she seems so bright, and she's gorgeous. *Maybe if I just fu...* I shake my head. No, she needs to stay far away from me.

From the first moment I saw her, I haven't been able to keep her out of my mind. It was when she danced into the kitchen, carefree and whistling an upbeat tune that would normally make me cringe, but instead I admired her honey eyes as they widened at the sight of me.

Then it was how heartbroken she was after Ian,

don't get me wrong I feel for her but the fact that I was jealous of her sulking about some idiot who doesn't deserve her freaked me out.

This isn't me. When I fuck around with a girl, it's normally for one night and I'm gone by morning, if not before. I haven't even touched this girl properly and she's invading my mind.

I've seen the way Emma looks at me. I know she's interested but I need to get away from her. She's a virgin; I'm not the guy who deserves to take that from her. But why does it bother me when I think about someone else touching her?

In quick strides, I battle with my heavy boots to make their exit.

Find someone else, Aiden, anyone else except her.

I make my way to the opposite end of the bar and consider ordering a beer, but I'm driving the girls tonight, so I need to relax on my own. I sit on the worn wooden bar stool, scanning the crowd for her even as I tell myself I should stop looking for her. *Maybe I can find a girl to dip my cock into, to get my mind off Emma and that short black dre—*

My thoughts come to a screeching halt when I see her standing alone. Ashley left her. I scan the crowd and find her dancing with some random dude. *Doesn't she have a boyfriend? Why would she leave Emma alone?* The thought infuriates me.

I watch as Emma's facial expression falls as she looks at Ashley and walks off the dance floor. Rising to my feet, I think about making my way to her. But I don't need to comfort her, I don't need to bother her. I want to, but I don't want to give her the wrong idea.

Not that I don't want to fuck her brains out and have her screaming my name until the sun rises. I have respect for the sweet girl and don't want to drag her into my bullshit.

Ashley is always talking about how amazing her roommate is and how happy she is to have a best friend she can trust. I don't want to hurt Emma and have Ashley mad at me. Hell, I've known her for a week, and I don't want to hurt her because she is so sweet and innocent.

Pure. That's the word I should be using to describe this girl. Even when she was humiliated by that fucking idiot, she felt a need to protect him, throwing herself over him only to be pushed away. An admirable trait if only she could find someone worthy of that level of loyalty.

The week has been interesting. My life usually consists of early mornings, business meetings, and locking down deals. I'm always on high guard, with the clients I work with dangerous things can happen in an instant. It's a nice change of pace to see my sister and relax, her and Emma have been a nice distraction. But I'm itching at the bit to return to the city. Money, my business, power, they await me, and they never disappoint.

A random guy grabs her waist and I jump to my feet, striding towards them without a second thought. As I get closer, I see her looking up at him and his ugly fucking polo shirt.

Why the fuck is she giggling at him? What did he say to her?

What am I even doing? They live here. This place is slap packed with college students. Maybe he's her friend. An old fling? No, that isn't her.

She grinds against him, and I can't stand the fucking sight of his grimy hands on her. I close the gap between us and grab the preppy idiot's shoulder firmly. He looks up at me with wide eyes. That's how most people react to me. Not Emma though, she hasn't judged me even once. But then again, most girls don't.

He stops moving as does Emma.

She turns around and her plump lips curl into a smile when she looks my way.

Is she trying to get a reaction out of me?

"Take your hands off my girl," I growl.

Emilia

I can't make out what Aiden said to the guy, but he releases me instantly. His irritated scowl and narrowed eyes follow as the stranger moves out of sight.

It isn't long before his brilliant green eyes focus back on me. With strong hands, he pulls me flush against him, my back to his front.

"What did you say to him?" I tilt my head back against his hard chest, leaning into him feels…natural.

"Don't worry about it," He whispers in my ear. "Dance with me," He instructs.

I oblige. Whatever he just did sent a wave of heat

through my body.

Riskier than usual with the alcohol in me, I slowly rock back and forth against him. We dance for a while, and when the beat picks up, so does my rhythm. I press myself back against him, grinding slowly. I feel something hard against my back, and it takes me no more than a second to realize what it is. I'm glad he can't see the blush rising on my cheeks.

"See what you do to me?" He whispers heatedly.

I try to think of a response, but our intimate moment is interrupted by Ashley. My eyes fly open. *Why did I close them?* Realization hits me that I'm dancing with her brother and I quickly fumble out of his grip that's still tight on my hips.

She laughs, putting her hand on my shoulder to steady herself. "Em! I don't care if you dance with him, I already told you to go after him." She drunkenly yells over the loud music.

Hearing Aiden laughing behind me, embarrassment crashes through me. I roll my eyes and grab her hand, leading her away before she says anything else. Aiden walks ahead of us, guiding us through the mass of bodies as we continue our tipsy trek.

A groan escapes my lips when I catch sight of Ian heading straight for us. I let go of Ashley's hand and instinctively step behind Aiden, my hands coming up to grip his shirt.

"What do you want?" Aiden's tone is venomous.

Vivid reality flows through me at the sight of Ian's face. Faded bruises cascade down his cheekbone. They're nearly gone after a week of healing, but I can still see how badly he was hurt.

Ian glares menacingly at him. They step towards each other with clenched fist, and I let out a breath I didn't realize I was holding as I think of how to diffuse the situation. Everything is happening so quick; I hate how alcohol does that.

Aiden reaches back and gently pushes me away. I become frantic at the thought of them fighting again. I don't want anyone getting hurt because of me.

"I'm going to pee," Ashley announces quickly before darting for the bathroom.

I roll my eyes. She's worse with confrontation than I am.

"Wait!" I shout, stepping in between them to keep them separated. "Ian, what do you want?" My words slur as I place my hands on my hips for support.

"I just want to talk." He eyes behind me. "Alone."

Aiden places a hand around my waist and tugs me into him. "Absolutely. Not."

Realizing it's a lost cause, I pull Aiden to the door. But he is like stone, an immovable force. Without thinking, I change plans and grab Ian, pulling him away. If Aiden won't go, I'll get Ian out of the situation. That way, no one can fight.

I glance back. Aiden looks pissed as he heads for the door but I'm thankful the situation didn't escalate.

I stop once I get to a quieter spot against the wall, but not wanting to go further away from people in the crowded club. I don't trust him.

"What do you want?" I tap my foot impatiently.

"I... I didn't mean what I said that night." His desperate voice clouds my ears.

I question if he truly means it. Then I remember his words from last weekend, clear in my mind that's fogged by alcohol. I turn on my heel and stomp away from him. A few steps away, I look back with the hardest glare I can manage.

"I just..." Unable to find the words for how over the situation I am, I sigh and muster up the courage to tell him just how I feel without making me sound like the wreck I am inside. "Don't contact me anymore, Ian. There's nothing more to say."

"Em. Wait, baby."

A bitter laugh escapes my lips. "Don't call me that." *How dare he.* "You don't have that privilege anymore," I hiss.

Turning on my heel, I make my way out to the exit.

Aiden

I kick a stray beer can hard, the clank echoing loudly in the alleyway. I had to walk outside. I'm fucking fuming. One minute she's grinding against me, making me hard, and the next, she's talking to fucking Ian.

Why do I care so much is the real question. I've only known her for all but one week, but the connection I feel with her is something I've never experienced before.

It isn't merely sexual, it's...primal.

I run my hands through my hair as I try to calm down. This isn't her fault. That stupid fucking frat boy hurt her, took advantage of her. And she is drunk.

What am I doing out here?

This guy's entire relationship with her was spent trying to get in her pants. She's vulnerable right now. I don't care if I need to stay away from her, I fucking can't.

I turn back towards the club and see Emma stumbling towards me. She looks so delicious in that dress. I don't usually give a fuck about girls.

But it's different with her.

I feel a need to protect her.

Five

The palms of my hands slam against the cool metal door and it swings out easily. A breeze hits my skin as I step outside. I stumble forth on tipsy legs, looking around for Aiden. I spot him leaning against his car, broodily.

"Aiden?" I study his face quietly.

His emerald eyes twinkle in the moonlight, rage sparking in them until his gaze meets mine. His distant expression softens, his edges quite literally turning putty.

I wonder if what Ashley said is true.

He holds his arms out and I walk into his embrace. He snakes his arm around my waist, pulling me tightly against him while he rests against his car. He firmly holds me in place, as if he's shielding me, protecting me from everything beyond him.

"Why did you come out here?"

"I don't know. I mean if you wanted to flirt, be

my guest," He grumbles, contradicting himself when he pulls me closer.

I roll my eyes. "Ian wanted to talk, and I told him to never contact me again. But why do you care?" I wonder if he'll admit he's interested.

He has to feel this connection we have; I know I do. I'm doing things I never do, like chase angry guys outside of clubs when I think they're upset with me. I even catch myself batting my eyelashes at this man.

Taking a deep breath, he tilts his face to meet mine. "Isn't it obvious? I haven't taken my eyes off you since I first saw you." His confession sends a swirl of butterflies through my stomach. His strong hands tighten on my hip, causing chills to rake down my body.

"I only talked to him because I was worried you would hit him." I mumble, looking away from his smoldering gaze.

He chuckles and lifts my chin, forcing me to meet his striking green eyes. "You don't need to worry about that."

"I didn't want you to get hurt."

And truthfully, I don't want Ian to get hurt. He may be an absolute idiot, but I don't like violence. Aiden is massive, and with him being so protective tonight, Ian could get seriously hurt.

His shoulders bounce from laughter. "I wouldn't be the one to get hurt, babe."

I blush at his bold choice of word. "I know but..."

A warm hand wraps gently around the nape of my neck, halting all rational thought. His gentle eyes bore into mine, as though seeking permission.

Hesitantly, I nod once, biting my lip. "You really should stay away from me." He tells me and then slowly, as if to not scare me away, he closes the distance between us. Our lips touch, light as a feather, soft as a whisper.

Anticipation fills me as I wait for our lips to collide.

"I should have punched Ian in the face!" Ashley's drunken declaration shatters the moment.

I sigh.

Aiden hesitates to release me as I wiggle away.

"Fuck," he curses under his breath, it's the first time I've seen his impenetrable persona slightly crumble.

Ash must not have seen us, or she doesn't care. She mumbles about Ian while yanking the front door of the car open.

I giggle as I watch her fumble into the seat. She's all talk, and no bite. Thinking about how she ran to the bathroom to get away from the situation makes me laugh harder.

"That's Emma's seat." Aiden states flatly.

I shoot him a warning glare, though secretly happy.

"Oh my God! You two can sit apart for five minutes. I swear you will live." She cackles at her joke before climbing over the leather seat and sinking into the back with a smirk.

I blush as Aiden smiles down at me before helping me into his car. I peek at the rearview to see Ash is already passed out as we take the short drive home.

Aiden's warm hand settles on my thigh and my body heats underneath his touch. I admire the way his large hand covers my leg. I bite my bottom lip when his fingers gently dig into my skin. Darting my glossy eyes in his direction, I note that his own glossy eyes are trained on me.

"Look at the road!" I chide quietly.

He laughs and tightens his grip on my leg, sending fire to my core. I bite my lip harder and he smiles, bringing his eyes back to the dark road ahead. We pull into the driveway seconds later, and he walks around to help me out.

"Can you pick her up?" I whisper, gesturing to Ashley who is now snoring away.

"I can carry you inside," He offers.

I shake my head and his shoulders slump.

"Fine." He sighs before gently lifting her off the backseat.

I stumble into the kitchen, in search of water, while Aiden brings Ashley to her room. I need something in my stomach besides liquor.

"Eat this." Aiden holds out an apple, I didn't even hear him walk into the kitchen.

"I'm fine. I'll just drink this," I gesture to my glass of water, pushing the apple away.

"Eat," He demands.

I roll my eyes at his commanding tone. I grab the apple and take a bite.

"Happy?" I ask sarcastically.

His eyes narrow darkly. "You should be happy

I'm not putting something else in your mouth right now."
He steps toward me as my mouth drops. He brings his
hand up, tapping my cheek. "Is this an invitation, babe?"

His dirty words make my body shiver
involuntarily.

"Wha...what?" I stutter.

"I'm trying to be nice, even though I'm still pissed
about Ian and the random dude you were dancing with.
So, don't push it." He states dryly.

"You don't own me," I huff, crossing my arms
over my chest.

"Point taken." Shaking his head as though to rid
all thoughts of me, he leaves the kitchen.

"Wait."

Aiden's sharp jaw is clenched but as his irate eyes
meet mine, he softens. "What? You said it yourself. I
don't own you. Go to bed." His tone is serious as he
gestures to the hallway.

"Fine." *Screw it.*

I spin on my heels and head for my room.
Shutting my door with a little more force than necessary,
I strip my dress off, throw on a big T-shirt and climb into
bed.

I fall into a light drunken sleep until my door
creaks open and my comforter is peeled off of me. As a
warm body snuggles up against mine, I tip my head back
to see Aiden's crooked grin.

"Thought you didn't want to be around me?" I

question sleepily.

"Don't push it," He warns, though I can tell he's teasing.

His warm breath makes my body tingle. He snakes his arm around me, his body heat warming every inch of my body. The sexual tension between us grows. At least to me, and I want him.

I grind against him like I did at the club and he grabs my waist, rocking back and forth, hardening against me. My breath quickens and I turn to face him.

I'm thankful for the moon as it casts a white glow around us, allowing me to take in Aiden's perfectly toned body. Ink covers his massive arms and part of his chest. His black hair is messy and he's wearing only grey sweatpants.

In a swift motion, he rolls on top of me. I gulp as I take in his intimidating size. His eyes take on a wild look as he brings his face to mine. Our lips crash together, and I sink my hand into his thick hair. His mouth expertly navigates mine as we kiss. First kisses are normally off, awkward, but the way I fit perfectly against Aiden's frame makes me feel protected and comfortable.

He rocks against me and I feel his hardness grazing the inside of my thigh. I moan as he pushes harder against me. I reach out to pull his sweatpants down, but he lifts himself off me the moment I grab them. My stomach drops.

"You don't want me?" I whisper through ragged breaths, embarrassed by how easy I must seem to him.

Aiden lays down beside me and cups my face. "I

want you too much. That's the problem. I want to rip your panties off and fuck you until you scream my name."

I shiver at his dirty, heated words. I know I should put more thought into who I give my virginity to, but I don't care at this point. Hell, I was about to give it to Ian. I would much rather lose it to Aiden.

I want him.

"Then what's the problem? Is it because I'm throwing myself at you? I'm not normally like this," I mutter under my breath.

"I know you're not normally like this. You're a virgin and shy at that, which means you want me a lot. Which in turn makes me want to fuck you more than I have ever wanted anyone," He states seriously. A sly smile crosses his face as he continues. "You're...I'm not going to take..."

I cut him off. "I'm capable of making that choice."

"You're drunk."

I can see the internal battle going on behind his eyes. "No... I'm sober now," I lie. I'm not completely drunk but I do feel a strong buzz.

"Let's just go to bed."

My heart squeezes.

He doesn't want me now. Why would he? I don't even know what to do.

"Why didn't you just take some random girl from the club home since you don't want someone inexperienced?" I huff and turn my body away, but his firm grip stops me. His deep chuckle irritates me more, and I struggle under his grip.

His eyes burn into mine. "Why would I want any of those sluts from the club?" He scoffs, eyeing me seriously. "Emma, look at you. You're fucking gorgeous. I can't control myself around you. I need you to be sober when I do anything to you. I will not do it when you're drunk."

He pulls me close and I snuggle my head against his chest. It takes me a long time to wind down and fall asleep as he plays with my hair.

I admire Aiden's now soft features as he sleeps. He looks less intimidating.

I wonder how he will be when he wakes up. Since he didn't drink, he obviously said what he wanted to with a clear mind last night. Still, I can't imagine why he's interested. He seems like the type of guy who needs a girl who is certain about her career path, not an inspiring chef who enjoys baking way too much.

I hope he gets up soon, so Ashley doesn't get upset about him sleeping in my room. A small voice reminds me that she doesn't mind. But after Ian, I need to take some time to myself, and keep my distance.

My mind scrambles to calm, always landing on the one haven I turn to. Baking. Maybe I'll make some pastries for breakfast.

I throw on a pair of shorts and head to the kitchen. I pull out the ingredients I need to make raspberry cheese Danishes. Pulling my hair into a messy bun, I plug my headphones in and work quietly.

Twirling around the kitchen, I take the raspberry filling off the stove to cool. Lost in the music, I stiffen when one gets pulled out. I turn, removing the other side, to see Aiden. His hair is a beautiful tousled mess, and he's still in his gray sweatpants that hang on his hips perfectly. A defined V draws my attention down his inked stomach.

I gulp.

"You're fulfilling my every fantasy," He murmurs, closing the small distance between us.

"What? Making breakfast with messy hair?" I laugh.

He wraps his arms around my waist and lifts me onto the cold countertop. The way he touches me feels natural. I've been trying to keep my distance but maybe…maybe I shouldn't.

"No, my fantasy of a woman in a kitchen dancing and making me food. The fact that you're drop dead fucking sexy only makes it harder for me to not take you over the counter here." He grips my thighs and taps a solitary finger on the marble countertop, emphasizing where exactly he will take me.

My breathing grows ragged and shaky.

"I know you want me, Em." His eyes burn into mine, his voice a soothing rumble. "I want you more, I can assure you of that. You don't have to play coy with me.

Six

Aiden leans in, trailing soft kisses down my jawline.

I wrap my legs around him. The exquisite feeling of his firm hands tightening around me as he lifts me off the countertop sends electric waves to my core.

He walks us toward the hallway, never taking his lips off my neck. "You're so fucking sexy, Em," He whispers into my ear.

A shiver runs through me. "I don't know ab—"

Ashley's door creaks open, cutting me off.

I scramble despite my legs still being locked behind Aiden's back. He chuckles and pulls us into the bathroom.

We share a silent laugh.

"Hey! I need to take a shower," Ashley demands sleepily.

Aiden studies me, setting me on my feet reluctantly. "Be out in a minute."

I reach for the doorknob once I hear Ashley's bedroom door close. A hand wraps around my arm and pulls me back just as the water starts running. The warm water causes steam to steadily build.

"I can't wait until my place is done. That way nothing can interrupt us," Aiden murmurs.

"I can't stay in here." *I don't really want to leave though.*

A dimpled smirk melts my protests.

"Shh, you'll be fine. Do you really want to go?" He slides his hands under my shirt slowly.

I give a shy shake of my head.

A smile creeps up his face, slight stubble trailing his sharp jawline.

"But…Ashley…"

"Don't worry. I won't be loud. Well, I won't be. But I'll have you screaming in a few minutes." He laughs as I playfully swat at him.

Sensually, Aiden peels my shirt off me, then my shorts, and finally my panties. My hands clench in nervousness as I'm slowly bare to Aiden's heated eyes. I think of stopping him, but the way he looks at me boosts my confidence. *I can be quiet.*

"Fuck," He mouths, holding his chin as though admiring an art piece.

I'm thankful for the thick steam obscuring my blush.

"Nervous?"

"A little." I peer up at him through batted lashes. This is all new to me, but when his hands are on me it awakens a natural drive inside that I never knew existed.

"You're adorable."

I let out a soft squeak when his large hands snake around the back of my thighs and lift me, though my legs wrap naturally around his waist. He carries me into the shower as I laugh at myself.

The moment turns into a frenzy of passion when he pushes me against the cool tiles, holding me in place. I feel him smile against my neck as he gently sucks and nibbles the sensitive skin there. The unfamiliar but welcome sensation of him growing harder against my bare skin excites me and I cover my mouth to hide my moans.

He pulls back, admiring where his lips just were.

"We have to be quiet," I remind through ragged breaths.

He hums in agreement.

A slight knock on the door alarms me.

"I'm going to skip the shower. I got to get going before traffic messes up my trip. Tell Em I said bye whenever she gets up!" Ashley yells through the door.

I hide a smile knowing we'll be alone any second, giggling when Aiden lets out a sigh of relief when the front door shuts moments later.

He eyes me intently. "Do you want me?"

I nod.

"Say it," He demands.

"I want you," I whisper shyly before bringing my

lips to his, affirming my words.

He glides one hand down to where my legs are spread, and I gasp. He pulls back to watch my expression as he glides a finger through my folds. I bite my lip at the forbidden touch. His eyes are on my lips as he slides a warm finger in a feather light motion across my aching clit.

I whimper when his hand transfers locations, until pleasurable moans escape my lips when his fingers twirl around my nipple. He gently kneads my nipple between his thumb and forefinger while he watches me turn to putty at his touch.

Sliding his hand down my bare stomach, he inserts one finger inside of me. "So wet for me," He growls, making me tremble within his strong arms.

I say nothing. I'm nervous of what's to come. Willing, of course, but very nervous.

He pumps his long fingers and I moan each time he goes a little deeper.

"I love that you're sitting on my hand right now." His eyes are wild as he takes in my euphoric expression. "You have no idea how badly I want to be inside of you."

"Please, Aiden," I beg.

He shifts underneath me, grabbing his massive length in one hand, and I gasp when I see him in all his glory.

He chuckles. "You sure you want to do this? I feel how tight you are. I don't want to hurt you."

His voice is sincere, but the sight of him stroking his length, getting himself ready for me pushes me over the edge. I throw caution to the wind.

"Please, I need you." My eyes plead with him. I've never experienced this want before, this lustful ache or attraction. I can feel the burning desire for him deep in my core.

His features darken as his breathing grows heavy. His voice is deep and filled with lust. "When I fuck you, you're mine. Got it?"

I hope his words are true. I can't think straight, and I'm wishing I was better equipped at sex.

"Yes," I finally say.

An encouraging chuckle escapes his lips. "Good girl."

He brings himself to my opening and barely gets the tip in before I let out a yelp, not expecting the discomfort.

He retreats instantly and I whimper at the loss. "Why did you stop?"

"I don't want to hurt you." His chest rises and falls quickly.

"I'll be fine. It'll hurt anyways, right?" I pout slightly, looking up at him innocently when he doesn't respond. "You don't want me?"

He bites his lip, sliding a hand around the nape of my throat. "You know better than that."

I dig my nails into his back and rock forward, satisfied when I hear him let out a soft moan.

"Later," He promises, bringing a solitary finger to my lips to silence me. "I want to take you properly. For now, let me make you feel good."

With that, he lifts my hands above my head and pins them down with one hand while the other slides down my body towards my core. His fingers push into me, stretching me, and I have to admit this is a much more comfortable feeling. I moan his name when his thumb strokes my clit while his long fingers simultaneously pump in and out of me.

"Fuck. I love it when you say my name," He rumbles into my ear before returning to lavish his attention on that spot on my neck. Moans spill from my lips as my body comes undone from the overwhelming pleasure his fingers bring, my legs shaking.

"Come for me," He demands.

And I do, just as his mouth crashes down on mine.

I smile as I wipe the steam from the mirror, watching as Aiden walks up behind me. He pulls my hair away from my neck and kisses the spot he's been paying a lot of attention to. When he lifts his head, I spot a large purple spot.

"Aiden! You gave me a hickey," I snap, thinking of ways to cover it up.

"Just marking what's mine." He smirks before kissing it once more.

I can't believe that just happened. I can still feel his hands on my hips, thighs, neck and between my legs. I shiver as I remember the pleasure he brought me.

Needing a way to collect myself, I throw on one of Ian's T-shirts over my tank top and a pair of soffee shorts before going to do my laundry. I'll burn his shirt once I have something clean and comfy to wear. But first, I need some coffee.

Aiden is leaned against the kitchen counter, flipping through some documents as worry lines crease his forehead. He's dressed smartly for work, all black of course. I take a moment to admire how his tattoos peak through. I've never thought much of tattoos before, but they are sexy on him.

I tiptoe around the kitchen as I get myself a cup of coffee, careful not to disturb him. However, my presence is made known when the mug slips from my hand and shatters against the hard tile.

Aiden looks up, his concentration turning to anger as he stares at me. He sets down the papers on the countertop and takes a deep breath.

"What the fuck is that?"

Taken aback by his unexpected anger, I frown slightly. "Umm...I'm sorry, it slipped."

He straightens, eyeing me. "No, sweetheart, not the mug." He gestures to me impatiently. "That shirt you have on. I know it's not yours."

"Oh, I didn't have any more clean clothes and Ian's shirt was all I had." I state nonchalantly.

He makes his way to me in two strides, emitting a deep, almost territorial laugh. He places his hand out and demands, "Off."

I take a step back and bump into the countertop. "It's just a shirt," I snap.

"You're mine." He growls, his eyes darkening.

Rolling my eyes, I slip it off, thankful I have a tank top on underneath. I watch as he takes it from me and chucks it into the trashcan with a smug look. I bend down to pick up the broken shards, but he redirects me to the counter before grabbing the dustpan and doing it himself.

"Come," He beckons me to follow and I oblige.

He can be demanding but that's what I like about him. He knows what he wants, and I'm more than happy to follow his commands.

He seats me on the armrest of the couch before laying his luggage out, revealing an array of neatly folded black T-shirts. He grabs one and slips it over my head, his fingers greedily stealing a touch of my skin as he does so.

I blush when he kisses my forehead and whispers, "Better." He gestures to the coat rack. "If you want it, my hoodie is over there. Wear it whenever you like."

The delicious scent of his cologne invades my senses making me dizzy.

"Thanks. Why did you get so jealous? It's just a shirt," I question out of curiosity.

He tucks a stray piece of hair behind my ear. "Remember our shower?" His warm hands make their way to the nape of my neck.

I nod as butterflies erupt in my stomach.

"I told you, you were mine. I meant it. I may have not gotten to fuck you properly, but I will. You're mine now. It's that simple." His voice is smooth like silk as he kisses his mark on my neck.

My body trembles with need as I eye the bulge in his pants. A sense of satisfaction washes over me, knowing that he wants me as much as I want him.

He uses his knee to nudge my legs apart as his mouth crashes down on mine, his tongue caressing mine. His knee presses against my core and I moan at the flash of pleasure. I'm surprised by how easily he turns me on. I rock my hips, grinding myself against his leg as whimpers escape me, begging him for relief.

He pulls away with a chuckle.

"Why did you move?" I whine, needing more.

He caresses my inner thigh, his thumb lingering dangerously close to where I want it to touch. "I'm going to be late for work if I stay any longer."

"When will you be back?" I blush, pressing my thighs together to alleviate the ache. I probably sound desperate, but I don't really care.

His smile grows. "You want me to fuck you, don't you?"

My eyes fall to the ground, embarrassed by his brazen words. "Umm..."

He cups my face gently. "I'll be back later," He promises. "You can hang out with Ashley when she gets home."

"She's gone for the next few days. That's why she was in a rush earlier and didn't shower." I remind him, blushing as images fill my mind.

"That's right." He hums in thought, his eyes

growing dark when he looks down at my fidgeting legs. "Wait, so you'll be here alone?"

I shrug. "Yeah, but I'll be fine. If I need anything, I have some friends down the street."

Crossing his arms, his eyes narrow. "Please tell me you're not going back to the frat house."

I bite my lip. "I'll know if Ian's around if his car is in the driveway."

He frowns in thought, carefully running a hand through his styled hair. "Wanna come to work with me?"

I twiddle my fingers as I ponder. It'd be better than having to sit and wait around all day. But can he just have people go to work with him whenever he wants?

"Is it okay if I go?"

"I'm the boss so...yeah." He pushes a stray piece of hair behind my ear.

With that, I run to Ashley's closet to change, picking out a simple summer dress and flats. It's nothing fancy but it's cute.

I stand in front of Aiden and twirl. "Is this okay?"

He bites his lip before nodding his approval.

"I'm sure you prefer high heels and tight dresses." I joke, curious about his preferences.

He places his hand on my cheek, and I lean into its warmth.

"I prefer this, I promise you." His eyes trail down my body.

"You looked hot as fuck at the club, but it was too revealing. I prefer this cute innocent look on you." He winks. "We can save the other stuff for my eyes only."

Seven

I slide into the Challenger, the leather seat is warm under my legs from basking in the morning sun. I love the classic feel of the car and the heavenly scent of leather mixed with Aiden's cologne. The engine roars to life and I watch in admiration as Aiden's muscles flex while he changes gears.

I turn the radio down and look to him. "When will your place be done?"

A half smirk forms on his face as he places a large hand on my thigh. "My apartment got finished yesterday."

"What? I thought it would be weeks." I droop a little, surprised and disappointed our time together is ending. "Why did you stay?"

"Isn't it obvious?" He grins wolfishly.

I look away with a blush.

His hand moves from my thigh to grip my chin, turning me back to face him. "It's adorable when you're shy."

I plaster on a smile. "Are you dropping me off at home and staying there tonight then?"

"That's where we are staying tonight." He winks, sliding his hand further up my dress as we drive along.

I eye the massive building in front of me curiously as Aiden helps me out of the passenger seat, handing his keys to the valet. His arm wraps protectively around me as we make our way into the lobby and towards the elevator. I look around, noticing the bottom floor is filled with men in business attire who are staring in our direction.

I glance at the directory by the elevator and my eyes widen.

Fortieth floor: Scott Investment Corporation.

Aiden gives me a cocky nod when I peer up at him. It's definitely something to be proud of, especially at the young age of twenty-five. I would be the same way too.

I giggle as he escorts me inside the empty elevator. "Why is everyone staring at you?"

He laughs. "They aren't staring at me."

Now it's my turn to laugh. "Right."

He cups my face. "That's what's going to get you in trouble. You don't know when men are flirting with you." He smirks before planting a kiss on my neck.

The soreness makes me jump and reminds me of something I forgot.

"I forgot to cover my hickey!" I shriek, embarrassed.

He shrugs, pulling my hair away from my neck so it cascades down my back, and admires his mark. "I would have wiped off any make-up you put on it."

His voice is so stern and authoritative, it makes me gulp.

The elevator dings and Aiden releases me, his features sharpening and growing cold. The doors slide open revealing a sleek and modern office design.

A woman sits at the white front desk, a bright smile plastered on her face. "Mr. Scott," She greets with a nod.

I return her polite smile when she looks over at me.

Aiden guides me over and introduces me to Lexi.

"Would you like some water?" Lexi asks with a smile.

I shake my head politely, not wanting to bother the nice lady. "I'm okay, thank you though."

"She'll have a water with lemon." Aiden instructs before guiding me towards the back of the room, his warm hand pressing into the small of my back.

The faint sound of heels and dress shoes against the marble flooring makes me stand a little straighter. A man hands Aiden a manila folder but they exchange no words.

I study them curiously. Is this how it will be like

when I work in an office one day? Everything looks so serious; from the white polished floors, ironed dresses to pressed suits. So different from my dream of being covered in flour all day, creating delicious treats with my hands.

This is what Aiden was born to do, his general no-nonsense demeanor shows more than usual. I can't deny that being next to him feels powerful and a little intimidating. I notice his voice sounds different when he talks to his employees, it's deeper, more serious.

My wide eyes take in the beautiful sight of Portland's skyline as Aiden ushers me into his office. The interior design is different from the rest of the floor; deep colors adorn the walls while rich oak furniture dominates the space. Fine-Art of various deep hues sit flush against the deeply colored walls. It fits Aiden.

Despite the natural light shining in through the floor-to-ceiling windows, he flips on a lamp that casts a faint golden hue over his desk. It looks incredible, like a luxurious cabin.

I spin around in awe. "How is everything so established? I thought you just got this place." I peer at the awards framed on the wall.

Aiden sits in the large leather chair behind a dark oak desk and powers on his computer. "This is the same set up I had when I went to Stanford and worked in the city. I already owned the company when I was in school, my employees just came with me. It's been an easy transition."

He beckons me over, pointing to his lap. "Come."

I shuffle over shyly and slide onto his lap sideways.

"We won't be here long." he twirls my hair as he taps away on his computer. "I just need to send some paperwork to my clients, and then we can head out."

The door opens and Lexi steps in, her bright smile fading.

I move to stand up, but Aiden holds me in place.

"Why didn't you knock?" He demands, his face set in a scowl.

"I'm sorry, sir." Lexi sets a glass down in front of me before making a quick getaway.

I tilt my head, puzzled. "Isn't it unprofessional for me to be on your lap?"

He shakes his head, his tone filled with disgust. "I'm the boss, I pay their wages. It was unprofessional for her to barge in here like that."

I push away my thoughts on the sadness I saw on Lexi's face. "Didn't you ask her to bring me water?"

He chuckles in amusement and leans back. "Okay, so let's say I had you bent over the desk," He taps the sturdy wood, "and someone just waltz in."

I blush as I picture him holding me down and taking me over his desk.

"Exactly." He nods. "This office is my sanctuary. Ms. Stone is skating on thin ice." He waves his hand absentmindedly.

"How so?"

He opens his mouth to answer, but stops himself. "I'm not sure it was a good idea to hire her on. She's…"

He shakes his head, planting a kiss on my bare shoulder.

I slide off Aiden's lap and explore his office, browsing the bookshelves that adorn the far wall. I trace the spines with Hemingway, Orwell, and Faulkner, making me put Aiden on more of a pedestal than before.

"All done." He turns off the screen.

I raise my brow. "Really? We've only been here for twenty minutes."

"Perks of being the boss." He smiles, gesturing to the door.

I point to the bathroom, letting him know where I'm headed. I see Lexi as I step in, her smile not as prevalent as it was before. I look at myself in the mirror, unable to stop from comparing myself to Lexi. Her golden locks are curled to perfection and she looks like Aiden's type. My concerns are answered when she turns to me with a scowl.

She crosses her arms as she examines me with beaded eyes before sneering, "You're not that special, you know."

I take a step back, stunned by her cruel words and confused at the same time. "Excuse me?"

She laughs as she scans my body. She rolls her eyes, throwing her blonde hair to one side. "Aiden brings his little toys around all the time. You aren't the first."

She turns to the mirror, puckering her lips. "Nothing to worry about," She murmurs.

"I don't understand why you're being so mean to me," I state quietly, uncomfortable with confrontation.

She titters, stepping towards me. "I came here for

Aiden. Don't screw that up for me. I know what he likes. I've seen the way he looks at me. He doesn't need some little girl like you, not with that body." With that, she leaves, the clicking of her high heels echoing in my ears.

I bite my lip, blinking back tears. Her words bring up some of my insecurities. I know I'm just a freshman in college who dreams of opening her own bakery. She may be a few years older than me and more established in her career, but so what?

Thinking of Aiden and her is way out of my comfort zone. I try to hide my emotions as I leave the bathroom. Aiden seems as drawn to me as I am to him. He wanted me to come here with him, or perhaps he felt guilty for leaving me alone?

Aiden's heavy footsteps break me from my thoughts. I wipe my eyes discreetly.

"What happened?" He demands.

I shake my head, not wanting to talk about it.

He cups my face, his voice soft and calming. "What happened, sweetheart?"

"Nothing," I whisper as a single tear rolls down my cheek.

His jaw clenches as he waits patiently.

I take a deep breath and gesture towards his office. Taking my hand, he guides me in as I figure out what to say. He lifts me up and sits me on the desk, planting himself between my legs.

I note the way his eye color changes when he's concerned. Light flakes of gold trace his emerald irises. "Please, Emma. Tell me what happened."

Another tear falls. "I don't want to sound immature," I admit.

He touches my cheek while his other hand rests on my leg. "Did someone say something to you?" His voice is laced with venom as his eyebrows crease.

I nod.

He stiffens. "Who?"

"Can we just go? It's not a big deal." I lie.

"Who?" He demands, bringing his face closer.

"Lexi," I admit.

He lets out a long breath. "What did she say?"

I hesitate, not wanting to cause trouble.

"Fine. You don't want to talk about it, that's fine. She made you cry, and that's all I need to know." He opens the door and calls someone over. "Ask Ms. Stone to come to my office, please."

I shake my head, not wanting to deal with her meanness again. Why can't I be more confident in myself? I should have told her off.

Lexi bounces into the room moments later, her face falling once she catches sight of Aiden and I.

The door is barely closed behind her when Aiden instructs coldly, "Get your shit and get out."

"But Aiden…" She whines.

He holds a hand up, cutting her off. I'm assuming from her words in the bathroom that this conversation isn't one of a boss and his employee, it's something deeper.

Crossing her arms, she looks around the room, "Can I at least explain myself?"

"There's no need. You aren't even on the payroll yet, so technically you're not a part of this company. I will not have childish drama inside my office. I should have never hired you in the first place."

Huffing, she stomps out of the room.

"I'm very sorry." His voice is soft and silky once again.

I love that he only speaks to me with that tone. "No, I'm sorry. I didn't mean to cause drama. I never do. I'm embarrassed I couldn't hide my emotions."

He laughs softly before helping me down and wrapping me in a tight hug. "I know you don't like drama. That's what I like about you."

I blush, thankful my face is buried in his chest so he can't see me.

"If anyone is ever mean to you again, don't hesitate to tell me." His voice is stern, but still filled with concern.

I nod in agreement as he pulls me away to wipe the tears from my eyes. "I didn't mean to get emotional. It just hurt to hear what she said."

"We'll discuss that later. You ready to go?"

The coast is clear as we head off. I'm thankful he stood up for me, but I just wish none of this happened. The first day I show up at his job, one of his employees gets fired because of me. How embarrassing. I wish I told her off and went on with my day.

I let out a long yawn as my eyes grow heavy, tired from the early morning. "Do you have a coffee machine at the apartment?"

"Yes, the realtor said it's completely furnished. But I haven't gotten a chance to get groceries, so no coffee."

"Want to go to a cafe? There's one near my new place."

I nod happily.

We pull up in front of the brick building that is swanky and different from the Dunkin Donuts by my place. Aiden pays for my large latte against my wishes, but I'm thankful. *I really need to get a job.* I look for a seat while Aiden waits for our drinks. I'm on my phone when the chair in front of me slides out and I look up to find a man in his twenties staring down at me.

He eyes me with interest. "Hey, mind if I sit with you?" Not waiting for my answer, he takes a seat.

"Actually..." I begin but I'm cut off when Aiden sets my latte in front of me.

"Hey princess." He scowls as he eyes the man. "Up," He demands.

I watch the stranger get up and walk away. "What was that about? He didn't know I was with anyone. Why are you so territorial?"

He laughs, covering my hand. "I told you, beautiful. You're mine."

Eight

It's dark out by the time we arrive at Aiden's new apartment.

His realtor greets us, handing Aiden his new keys. "Hello Mr. Scott, I hope you and your..." She trails off as she looks at me, extending her hand with a warm smile. "I'm Paula. It's nice to meet you!"

I return her handshake. "I'm Emma. It's my pleasure."

Aiden's lips curve into a small smile at my formality.

"Mr. Scott, your apartment is fully furnished. If you have any issues, please do not hesitate to call me."

"Thank you very much, Paula." Aiden guides me into the elevator and pushes the button to the penthouse.

The elevator door opens, and I'm taken aback when I see a large open living room. I had expected a hallway leading to multiple apartments.

I look at Aiden in surprise. "This whole floor is one apartment?"

He laughs as he undoes his cuffs. "Of course, it is. It's a penthouse." He throws his jacket on the rack. "I'll be back in a moment. I'm going to hop in the shower. Wanna join?" He winks.

I shake my head.

"I ordered us food. It should be here any moment." He calls out as he leaves.

I take in the modern and masculine architecture. The white floors and walls contrast with the black leather furniture that adorns the living room. The kitchen and dining room have a similar setup, but what truly takes my breath away is the view. The city skyline is so close.

The chime of the doorbell echoes throughout the house. With a grumbling stomach, I dash to the door to retrieve our food. I wonder what he ordered.

A man stands on the other side of the door, empty handed. He's covered in tattoos and is as tall as Aiden. He's not as muscular but he's still pretty fit. He looks off, scary even. His eyes rake up and down my body as he stands in silence. He definitely isn't the deliveryman.

"Can I help you?" My voice trembles slightly. Alarm bells go off in my head when he remains silent. Ashley's voice reminding me that Aiden works with bad men penetrates my brain.

I attempt to slam the door shut, but he slaps a large palm against it and pushes it open with ease. The gesture frightens me, and I jump, letting out a slight yelp.

Where is Aiden?

I watch as the stranger paces around the room before coming to stand in front of me, a little too close for comfort. Dad was a police officer and I often listened to him tell Mom about certain cases. I note his demeanor. He isn't twitchy or sluggish, so no drugs. Angry and paranoid? Yes.

I back away, attempting to head towards Aiden's room but he pushes me against the wall.

"Where is he?" The stranger demands. His voice has an accent. Italian, maybe?

"In...in the...bathroom," I stutter, hoping he will be out of there soon.

The man smiles creepily at me, tucking a lock of hair that fell out of place behind my ear. "Maybe I can take you for payment."

I shudder at his touch and stiffen in fear. My mind races, but my worries melt away when I see a pissed off Aiden stalking his way towards us. His dark hair is wet from the shower and he only has gray sweatpants on.

Aiden yanks the man away, pinning him by his throat. His eyes darken as he holds the man in place.

I let out a sigh of relief.

"Se la tocchi di nuovo, ti ucciderò." His voice is deep and full of venom.

I try to decipher Aiden's words but he's speaking in another language. Italian, definitely Italian. I wish I could understand what he was saying.

"Sweetheart, can you go to the balcony for a moment? And don't look inside." His voice has softened but it still holds a note of anger.

I nod, more than happy to get away from whatever is going on. I slam the balcony door shut behind me. But the anticipation is too much, and it isn't long before I'm peering in.

Aiden throws the man on the floor once I'm out of the danger zone. He glances over at me and gestures for me to turn around. I obey for a moment but worry fills me and I turn my head slightly to keep an eye on him. I watch with wide eyes as they yell at each other, and all too quickly, a fight ensues. It doesn't last long as Aiden punches the man in his jaw, and he falls limp onto the floor.

Aiden makes a quick call on his cellphone and looks up to see me staring. He quickly makes his way to me. His breath is ragged, and I can see his hands trembling.

"I thought I told you to look away."

I step back instinctively. I'm not scared of him, but his voice is so deep and authoritative that it frightened me. I don't say a word.

He shakes his head. "I'm sorry." His voice gentle once more. "I'm not mad at you. I just didn't want you to see that. Don't fear me. Please."

"Who is he?" I nod at the large unconscious man.

Aiden wraps me in a hug, he hesitates before speaking again. "Casualties of the job."

I wonder how dangerous his life is. "Am I safe here?" I whisper, the tremble in my voice is clear.

He tightens his hug. "Of course, you are. He

shouldn't even know where I live, but he found out somehow. I'll make sure to put security guards by the elevator and the downstairs lobby, so this never happens again," He promises.

A knock sounds on the door moments later, which Aiden answers. A few commands are spoken, and a man slings the stranger over his shoulder and makes his way out silently.

I wonder how Aiden handles this so well. This must be normal for him, this life…but my trembling hands send warning shivers throughout my body.

Our food arrives shortly after. I watch as he unboxes countless boxes slapped full of Thai food. My stomach growls in anticipation but I'm too shaken up.

"Eat." He looks at me with concern. "I'm sorry about that, but everything's okay. Let's eat and talk about it, okay?"

A silent dinner ensues, as I debate over what to say. Can I leave after how quickly sparks have flown? Even though his life may be full of danger, can I ignore our chemistry?

Finishing my food, I eye him curiously. "What did you say to that guy? I didn't know you spoke Italian." I realize there are a million things I don't know about him yet.

He leans back in his seat, taking a swig of his beer with casual ease. "Sure you want to know?"

I nod.

He places a hand on mine. "I told him if he ever touched you again, I would fucking kill him." His voice is calm and collected.

I chuckle. "You wouldn't really kill someone for me, would you?"

He straightens as his green eyes pierce mine. "Emma, I know we just met, but I don't give a fuck about what is normal when it comes to you. There is nothing I wouldn't do to ensure your safety. Absolutely nothing."

The way his eyes narrow in a sensual way makes my heart almost burst out of my chest, but should I think twice about this? Is this someone that I need to get involved with? "That really scared me. That man…" I trail off, shaking a shiver from my body.

He wraps his hand around mine, "I know." He looks down, biting his lip. "Nothing like that will ever happen to you again, I promise." I throw caution to the wind, ignoring every ounce of my mind telling me to run as I look up at him with batted lashes.

***

He takes my hand in his and leads me up a stairwell. My confusion fades when he opens the door and reveals a rooftop patio. My breath catches as I take in the sight of stars overhead twinkling in the night sky, a rare sight in a city. The twinkling lights are a well needed distraction from the events of the evening.

Greenery lines the balcony while subtle warm light cascades down from the circular bulbs, creating a very romantic ambiance. My eyes trail to a small outdoor bed where plush white sheets lay on top. I gulp in nervousness, imagining how perfect it would be to lose myself in him in such a romantic setting.

He picks me up without a word and I wrap my legs tightly around him. His grip is firm on my ass as he heads for the outdoor bed. He lays me down and hovers over me. His massive frame hides the starry sky, but I don't complain. He's a much more glorious sight.

I run my hands through his thick hair, ignoring everything that happened, as our bodies and lips collide. My insecurities creep in no matter how hard I try to push them away. I was just cheated on, and I'm paranoid. Even though Aiden makes me feel beautiful I fear I'm not exactly his type.

"Look." Aiden looks down, the night casts shadows on his sharp jawline sending a frenzy of chills through my aching body. "I don't want to sound stupid, but you can have any girl you want. I'm not special, or established, or anything. I don't want you to sleep with me and take my virgin…you know…and never talk to me again."

He plants a kiss on my forehead. "Em, I told you that you're mine. I don't give a fuck about anyone else. I never have. You've seen the way I am with you. I've never let a girl stay the night where I live. I wanted you the moment I saw you. I wanted you to be mine, no one else. End of story. This is the first time I've ever felt this way for someone. So, when I take your innocence, that's it for you…and for me. You'll simply be mine."

My body melts at his words. I can sense his sincerity and honesty. I've seen the way he treats others, with disinterest. But he's different with me. He wants me to be his, and I want that too.

"There is one thing though. This is a one-time thing." He circles his finger. "This sweet, romantic side of me in bed. When I take you for the first time...when I take your innocence," His breath grows ragged, and I feel him harden against me. "It won't always be this way. I'm going to fuck you rough once you get used to me."

I nod, my breathing growing fast. I don't care what way he wants me. He can have all of me.

He grinds against my core, his hard length pushing against my slit through my panties, making me ache for him. His hands are wild against my body as they squeeze and caress me.

His lips collide to mine, our tongues in a warm dance as his hand holds my face possessively. He pulls off my dress in one quick and impatient movement, his eyes wild and hungry, before stripping his own clothes off.

My eyes trail down his bare, tattooed chest to his groin. The size of him still surprises me. I don't know how he's going to fit. I wrap my hands around his hot length, barely covering it, and give it a tentative stroke.

"Your hands look good on me." A deep growl resonates in his chest, he watches my movements with hooded eyes. "This may hurt."

The incessant buzzing of my phone ruins the moment as Aiden peppers kisses along my jawline. I move my hand around blindly, trying to hit ignore but I just can't hit the right buttons.

Frustrated, Aiden leans over and grabs my phone. His body grows stiff and he turns the phone to me. Ian. "Why the fuck is he texting you?"

I shrug. "It doesn't matter. I'll block him later. Can we continue?" I plead.

He looks as though he wants to jump through the phone and kill Ian.

"Are you mad at me?"

"Of course not, it's just…you're mine." He states, tossing my phone on a nearby chair and looms over me. "I don't want your ex texting you. He's fucking nothing." His jaw clenches while his eyes look almost animalistic. "I'm going to prove to you why he doesn't matter. Why no man matters, but me."

I'm angry at Ian for making him upset, but the territorial way Aiden looks at me is making me feel things…really good things I've never felt before.

I hide a smile. "I know no one matters but you."

He kisses and sucks on my neck more aggressively than before. I'm a little startled by my voice, smooth and full of want.

"I don't know why no one's ever fucked you, but I'm glad they didn't. I get all of this to myself. Do you know how happy that makes me? How fucking turned on I am by your innocence?"

I involuntarily let out a moan as his mouth trails my neckline.

"Just say the words, and I'll fuck you, Em."

I nod eagerly, staring at him with hopeful eyes.

"Say it. I need to hear how much you need me

inside of you." His usual emerald eyes are a deep jade from lust.

"I want you, Aiden," I whisper through ragged breaths. I want him so badly. Can't he tell how much I need him?

He trails kisses down my body, starting with my lips, then my neck, and stomach. His movements are wild and uncalculated as he moves down until he reaches my panties. He smirks devilishly as he pulls them down carefully. Gripping my trembling thighs in his warm hands, he peels them open slowly. I feel exposed, but the way he admires my body makes me feel confident.

He slides a long finger up my slit and caresses my clit. I shake beneath his touch. He lifts his finger to his mouth and licks it clean. "Fucking delicious." He murmurs, bringing his face down.

I close my legs, surprised.

"Too fast?" He looks concerned.

"I've never done this before."

"Really?" He sounds excited, intrigued.

I nod.

"Open for me, baby. It will feel good," He coaxes.

I push past my nerves and spread my legs for him. I tremble as he expertly circles my clit with his tongue. The feeling is exquisite, so warm and euphoric. I moan as his tongue plunges deeper, exploring me. I writhe beneath his touch, collapsing further into the soft bedding. Blissful minutes pass by as I'm in euphoria, his thick hair clenched between my fingers.

He brings his free hand slowly up my stomach, I gasp when he twirls my nipple between his warm fingers. Another new sensation spreads through me as I admire his back muscles while both of his hands work magic on my body.

"Come for me," Aiden commands, replacing his mouth with his warm fingers. His long fingers strum my clit perfectly, sending waves of pleasure through my body. He watches with a smirk, as I come undone with a moan of his name.

Still trembling, I cover myself up with my hands, embarrassed by how intimately he's seen me.

Aiden lets go of my thighs and pins my arms above my head. "Don't cover your body. You're fucking perfect." He kisses me deeply before nibbling my ear. "Are you ready for me, beautiful?"

"Yes, please," I whisper.

He rubs his length through my slit, sliding it up and down, teasing me but not entering.

"Aiden, please," I beg.

"I needed to make sure you're wet enough."

He pumps his length in one hand as he grabs a condom from his pants, ripping it open with his teeth. I admire how he puts it on, having never seen it done in person.

Lowering himself, he nudges the head of his cock against my opening. I wince as I feel him stretch me. He pushes in slowly, stopping to make sure I'm okay. I rake my nails across his back, eliciting a pleasurable moan. He presses in again. This time, it's better, but I shift around.

"Shh, it will be over soon. The pain will turn into pleasure," He coos as he continues his small rhythmic thrusts until he finally fills me completely.

"So fucking soft."

I moan as his thick length stretches and fills every inch of me. The stinging pain subsides and is replaced by an overwhelming pleasure. The sound of skin against skin, his kisses and moans send me into a euphoric state.

He catches my moans in his mouth, then he nibbles on my bottom lip. "You're so fucking tight, baby." Aiden groans, cupping my breasts. Holding them firmly, he speeds up his thrusts, going harder.

I moan his name, and I can tell he likes it because his deep moan turns into a growl as he thrust deeper inside of me. His large hand grips my hair as he dives into me, sweat glistening off his skin.

"I'm going to come," He growls, his breathing ragged. His hands hover over every inch of my skin, he grips and squeezes in all the right places.

A whine escapes my lips when he pulls out. I want more of him, I need him. I watch, confused and enthralled, as he removes the condom before pumping his length. With a groan, he spills himself on me, marking me.

I look down at the sticky substance, panting as my legs tremble. I wonder why he didn't just cum in the condom?

"Fuck." He moans, placing his warm hands on me. Lowering himself down to place his forehead on mine, he grins. Planting gentle kisses along my face, his minty breath tingles my skin.

We admire each other and the breathtaking city skyline as we cuddle on the rooftop.

Nine

I jolt awake as a female voice booms through the apartment. My eyes squint at the bright glare of light filtering into the room. The unfamiliar bedding alarms me until realization floods me of where I am.

After Aiden made love to me, we took a shower together and then we snuggled up in his bed talking for hours. I still can't believe how perfect everything was.

The voice gets closer, more recognizable. "Wake up, bitch!"

Oh no! Ashley's back from her trip.

I scramble. My hands grasp for Aiden but come up empty, except for a small note by my pillow. **I'm gone until tomorrow, stay out of trouble.** I roll my eyes at the short message. Why didn't he wake me up to say goodbye?

The door swings open and Ashley marches in. "Oh my God."

Rolling my eyes playfully, I fall dramatically back onto the silk bedding. "Shut up."

She hops onto the bed, throwing her head back in a fit of laughter as she falls beside me. "I can't believe you're here…in his bed. He let you stay? What is happening to my brother!"

I look over at her and throw my hands up in innocence "Nothing happened."

She shakes her head. "Truly, I don't want to know." She saunters over to the drapery and throws them open, revealing the morning view of the bustling city below.

Grabbing my dress, she tosses it to me. "Take my brother's shirt off and get dressed. We're going out tonight and we need new clothes." She dangles a black credit card between her fingers, a mischievous sparkle in her eyes.

"Out?" I'm unsure if I want too. Aiden did say to stay out of trouble.

She peels the covers back. "Yes, out. Now, up!"

I gesture for her to leave the room, not wanting her to be stuck with a vision of her brother and I that she won't be able to get out of her head.

Now that Ash stepped out, I can reminisce on last night. My body may be a little sore, but Aiden handled me with so much care that my heart flutters when I think about it.

After we finished making love, the sheets were ruined. I was embarrassed and felt guilty for destroying his crisp white bedding, but he handled everything with such maturity that it made me realize, this is a man and how a man is supposed to treat a lady.

He wrapped me in the clean top sheet and took his time collecting our things and bundling up the other sheet to dispose of it. It was full circle; I gave him my virginity and he gave me the respect of not embarrassing me about the blood. He didn't even flinch, as a real man should.

We showered together, silent but perfect as he swiped the soapy loofah across my skin, planting kisses as he rinsed me off. It was the first night I saw him let his guard down, his full dimpled smile graced me last night and my only fear now is him pulling that away and returning to the serious man he normally is.

The rooftop was decorated so beautifully. Aiden made losing my virginity the most romantic experience of my life, what I always dreamed it would be. I shouldn't word it as a loss, as I don't see it that way. No, it's a gain. A new exploration of myself and I trust Aiden to hold it with respect, my first gift to him.

I spot a note on top of a blue box on the dresser. **I had my shopper grab these for you. They're for my eyes only. By the way, I'm only a town over. So, if you need me, just text me. Last night… it was fucking perfect Emma. I'll be back before you wake up tomorrow, and again…stay out of trouble.**

So, his first gift to me. I open the box to find a matching set of lingerie. I slip it on, seeing as I have nothing else to go under my dress. The lace is soft against my skin. I find myself tracing the places Aiden's hands had been last night, longing for him to be back.

I sigh and slip my dress on before heading out. I find Ashley in the kitchen, surrounded by trays of food, fruits, pancakes, bacon and eggs. It looks like a breakfast buffet.

Ashley picks up a piece of paper and reads it in a deep voice, mocking Aiden. "I wanted to make sure you ate while I was gone."

I laugh as I snatch the note away, moved by the sweet sentiment. I sit down and happily dig into the delicious food.

"What did you do to him?" She teases, as she walks around the spacious kitchen, admiring Aiden's new apartment. She tosses a grape into her mouth. "I missed you so much."

Walking around the bar top, I throw my arms around her neck. "I missed you too. How did it go with Brian?"

She flicks her wrist in the air dismissively. "Awful, I'm over him. That's why I need a girl's night. Plus, we're in the city, which means better clubs!" She cheers, sliding my fake ID across the marble countertop.

"I don't know, Ash," I hesitate, sliding it back to her, unsure what Aiden will think.

"I'm not taking no for an answer. You may be staying here and doing God knows what with my brother, but you're still my best friend and I have the power," She declares.

We glide through moderate traffic thirty minutes later, arriving at a swanky boutique.

"So why are we here?" I run my hands along the fabric of a navy-blue dress. My fingers clasp against the price tag as I turn it to her.

She doesn't flinch. "Shopping," She states in an obvious tone. She pulls out the black card from her wallet and dangles it. "It's Aiden's."

I shake my head. "You can use it, but I'm not."

"He said you would say that." She laughs. "I promise he gave me this card specifically for us to get something nice to wear tonight," She assures.

I relax a little. I don't want to spend his money, but if he insists.... Plus, I'll wear it all the time.

"He knows we're going clubbing?" I'm a little disappointed he doesn't care if I party without him. I kind of like his jealous side.

"Not exactly..."

I roll my eyes, waiting for her to elaborate.

"He may have specifically told me we aren't allowed to go "out-out", so I may have told him we're going out for a really nice dinner. Which we are! He made the reservations, but after that...we're going out!" She grins and shrugs. "What he doesn't know won't hurt him."

I'm already thinking of a million ways to cancel tonight.

"His driver is taking us to dinner, but we will just get out of that." Her grin is mischievous.

After hours of shopping, we stuff our bags into her backseat and make our way back to the apartment. I spy the guard from last night talking to a woman I don't recognize; her scarlet hair is perfectly curled as it lays against her crisp and skintight white dress. The dress is short, more suited for a night out. She huffs as she makes her way towards the exit.

Ashley hands me her bags and runs off. "I can't wait until we get up to the room. I have to pee now!"

I catch the lady's ramblings as she hurries past me. "I'll just fucking call Aiden myself."

I grab her elbow instinctively, surprising myself. "Aiden?"

She stops, tilting her head to the side as she studies me. She raises her brow, a fake white smile plastered on her face. "Yeah, you know him?"

"Yeah." I frown. "Why do you want to talk to him?" I ask in a venomous tone, my cheeks burning as jealousy floods through me. She could be a business associate or something, I need to calm down.

She crosses her thin arms over her chest and looks down at me. "He was supposed to have me over last night, but he never called." She pouts. "Be a doll and tell him to call me. My name's Rebecca." Smiling, she turns on her heels and heads for the door. Her brilliant red hair bounces as she exits, the color matching my mood.

Anger boils deep inside of me. She was supposed to stay the night with him. How much betrayal can I handle? What's worse now is that we shared the most intimate moment of my life. No one has ever seen me the way Aiden did last night. But he's seen plenty of girls, who spread for him probably nightly. How am I special?

I'm not.

I try to hide my anger when Ashley returns. The guard escorts us onto the elevator. I straighten myself up and plaster on a smile. *Screw it, I'm going out tonight.* We obviously aren't exclusive so who is he to say what I can and can't do?

I lean into Ash, so only she can hear. "So what club are we going to?"

Aiden

After a million handshakes and talks of business investments, I wonder how long this meeting will last.

My meetings usually take place in an office, yet here I am, a whole city away from Emma in an overly lavish home. I didn't want to deal with the pointless conversations and the sleazy women these men throw around to help them secure high-profile investment deals, but it is a big account.

I check my phone when it buzzes with a text. *Why did the girls refuse my driver?* The thought of Emma being out at night in the city without protection pisses me off. The driver I hired doubles as security.

I step onto the balcony and call the restaurant to see if they made it to their reservation. Lighting a cigarette, I calm when I hear that they're there. I wonder what Emma bought today. I hope she didn't refuse my offer to pay. I know from Ashley that she and her mom get by on the little money her mom's florist shop makes, and the thought of her doing without upsets me.

I hope she likes the lingerie set I got her. I found them online this morning and sent my shopper to fetch it for her. Imagining her wearing what I bought her makes my dick get hard. She's so fucking sexy and innocent. The things I want to do to her drives me fucking wild, but I need to be patient.

I pinch the bridge of my nose, remembering the call from my guard earlier about a woman trying to find me, probably from my late nights in the city back when I was doing business in Portland while in college. I don't even know which one of those crazy women showed up at my apartment. I just moved there, so why does everyone know where I fucking live? Someone is leaking information and I have a suspicion it may be Lexi. I need to deal with that first thing tomorrow.

My jaw clenches when I read the next text that arrives.

Mr. Scott, your sister just arrived at the club. Would you like me to seat her and her friend in VIP?

Absolutely fucking not. She's supposed to take Emma to get a new outfit and then to dinner, not to a fucking club. I slide the phone into my pocket and head for the door.

"Mr. Scott! The night just started. Where are you heading off too?" A woman in a short-glittered dress calls out as she glides over.

"Someone's in trouble," I state absentmindedly as I pull my keys from my pocket.

"Oh, I'm sorry. Anything I can do to help?" She

skims her finger along my blazer while fluttering her eyes at me.

I grab her wrist and move her disgusting hands away. "No, no not in trouble as in harmed. But she better pray that I calm down by the time I get to her."

I push past, shaking a few hands and thanking them for having me. I try to temper my anger as I slide into my car and haul ass to the club. The club that I own.

After a mess of hairspray and make up, we walk out of the penthouse, ready for a night out.

I have on the royal blue dress I bought earlier; it's tighter and shorter than what I normally wear, but I bought it with the intention of wearing it for Aiden when we go out to dinner or something. I frown at the thought. Maxon, Aiden's driver, is supposed to take us out tonight, but we opt out so smoothly I don't think he's aware we're up to something.

Our first stop is an Italian restaurant. The ambiance of the place is beautiful; warm light cascades over the thick white tablecloths. There aren't as many tables as I'm used to at a restaurant. We're ushered to a very private spot upon arriving.

We can barely read the words on the menu and laugh at how ridiculous it all is. But when the food comes and everything melts in our mouths, we quickly declare it as our new favorite place. The waiter even told us our meal will be put on Mr. Scott's tab and to enjoy the rest of our night.

I'll thank Aiden for the beautiful scenery and food, if I ever speak to him again.

Who am I kidding? He's all I can think about. Every time someone passes by in a black suit my heart races as I peer from the corner of my eye, hoping it's him.

I shake my head; I should be mad at him. He used me. He had planned on having another girl at his place last night. *Was I not special to him?*

I chug down the remainder of my wine.

Our fake IDs aren't necessary here, but I'm thankful they don't bother to card us. It makes me feel more grown, more like a woman, more on par with Aiden. It gives me the confidence to go to the club and flirt with every guy to take my mind from him. No one owns me; I can do whatever I want.

It's not like Aiden will ever find out anyways.

"So where is this club?" I look down the dark street while Ashley fixes her hair and smooths down her dress, putting my hand out to hail a cab.

Ashley grabs my hand and leads us down the sidewalk. "Just a few blocks over." She claps as we make our way through the dark streets.

I stumble, trying to keep up with her long legs. How does she walk so quickly in heels? I glance down at my black stilettos, a thin strap wrapping around each ankle.

A long line wraps around the front of the club, but Ashley heads for the front door.

"What are you doing?" I watch the line speed by at a dizzying pace as we rush past.

"Seeing if we can just go straight in." She winks as we walk up to a huge bouncer, who scans us both, a sleezy smirk spreads across his face.

"Welcome ladies." He undoes a silk ribbon from a post and ushers us in. The thumping of music, flashing lights and fog fill the night as the steel door opens.

I drag Ashley to the bar, needing to forget Aiden and the pain in my chest. The bartender greets us promptly, and I look over at Ashley. "I'm drinking tonight. Order whatever will get me absolutely wasted." I may be overreacting, but I thought he really liked me, but now that I know another girl is within reach it makes me feel like he's a player. But he said I was his? What if that was just dirty talk?

She shoots me an odd look, but a wide smile plays on her face before she slides Aiden's black card across the black countertop. "Tequila, double shots. Keep them coming and open us a tab please."

The first shot hits me hard, and I'm thankful we ate earlier and had a nice walk to settle my stomach. My throat burns, but after the second shot, a soothing warmth spreads to my stomach.

"Calm down, tiger." Ashley jokes as she slides a third shot out of my reach.

I pout. I notice a man dressed in a suit watching Ashley from across the bar. His head is tilted to the side, as though curious.

"Don't look now but someone is eyeing you," I murmur as I reach for the shot, downing it before Ash can stop me.

"Who?" She asks, thankfully not turning around because he's making his way towards us.

"He's walking over here. Act natural." I fumble, trying to quietly flag down the bartender. I need another drink.

"Ashley Walters?"

Now that the man is closer, I can see his features better. He looks sweet, not covered in tattoos, with a hint of scary but very sexy.

Why am I thinking of Aiden right now?

I study the guy. He's tall but not as tall as Aiden.

Why am I comparing him to Aiden? I need more alcohol.

"Oh my gosh! Ricky!" Ashley screams, jumping into his arms and pressing a kiss to his cheek.

I spot a small metal name tag on his suit. *I guess he works here.*

Ashley pulls me close. "Em, this is Ricky. He is Aiden's only friend."

Seriously? Why is he freaking everywhere?

They laugh but I can tell Aiden probably doesn't have many friends.

"What are you doing here?"

He gestures to the name plate. "I work here?"

"I didn't even know you lived here!" Ashley leans against him, the alcohol clearly taking effect. I get lost in my own mind while they catch up, tilting my head to my left I note a figure looming nearby. His dark eyes are trained on me for a moment, I shift in my seat uncomfortably. He's young but I can't tell if he's checking me out or if he has ulterior motives. I know Aiden told me after the incident at the penthouse to always keep a watchful eye out. So, I turn my body back towards Ricky and Ash, trying to ignore the bad feeling in my gut.

I watch Ricky pull out his phone and tap on it. After a while, he shrugs and shoves it back in his pocket. "Do you ladies want a VIP booth?"

We turn to each other before nodding our heads eagerly. We giggle as he takes us upstairs and into a private room. There's a leather couch with a table in the middle. A silver bucket filled with ice sits on the table and a champagne bottle sweats on top.

"I'm not going to ask how you got in here, but just be careful tonight, okay? If you need anything, come find me." He looks at Ashley intently, caressing her cheek.

She twirls her hair, her signature flirting technique, and nods.

Ricky corks the bottle for us before he walks out, sneaking glances at Ash a few times.

"He is wayyyy cuter than I remember," Ashley gushes as she turns to me.

"It's probably the alcohol, but I agree, he's cute."

We laugh as we pour the bottle of champagne into long-stemmed glasses.

With half the bottle gone, we stumble onto the dance floor. My vision is blurred but I find myself swaying to the rhythmic beats.

Time moves so much faster than normal, and before I know it, I'm grinding against someone, his strong arms grip my waist as we sway back and forth. I catch a glimpse at the guy behind me. He looks nice. Curly brown hair and blue eyes smile at me as I continue getting lost in the rhythm.

I feel a loss of contact, but before I can turn around, the strong arms return and they're tighter around my waist. He slinks his arm around, hugging me from behind.

I look down and see a familiar trail of ink on tanned skin.

"What the fuck are you doing?" A familiar husky voice asks.

Ten

I turn around slowly, meeting a set of fiery, emerald eyes. Aiden's face is set in a deep scowl as I look at him inquisitively.

Did he lie about the meeting tonight? Has he just been out partying?

I look around for the guy I had been dancing with and find his body on the floor. People are staring in our direction.

What did I miss? What just happened? Most importantly, why is Aiden here?

His scowl turns into a cocky smirk. "Surprised to see me?"

I nod slowly. "Ho…how did you…find me," I slur.

His brow furrows. There's no amusement in his tone. "Are you drunk?"

"No." I lie but I stumble on my heels.

Aiden steadies me, heaving an annoyed sigh before guiding me to the bar.

The bartender places a shot in front of me within seconds.

I go for it, but Aiden slides it down the bar top, causing it to spill over the black surface. He's going to get us kicked out.

"Chill, Aiden," I slur.

"If you hand her one more sip of alcohol, I will fire you for overserving customers." His voice is stern and laced with venom as he eyes the frightened bartender.

How can he fire him?

Aiden looks intimidating as he crosses his arms. "On a better thought, how much did you serve her?"

"Mr. Scott, I…I didn't–"

He cuts him off with a wave of his hand. "Did you even check her… Fuck it, you're fired. Get out of my sight." He beckons another bartender, who quickly makes his way to us, and demands, "Water."

A glass of water is placed in front of me moments later and I slowly sip it as the room spins. *Why does Aiden own a bar? Oh right, investment properties.*

Warmth spreads through me as he places a possessive hand on the nape of my neck. I remind myself that I'm still mad at him.

"Ge…get your hands off me!" I hiss.

He laughs lowly. "What did you just say to me?"

"I said," I attempt to stand but his hand holds me in place, sending a shiver through my body. I hate that I like it when he's like this, and the alcohol is not helping. "I said get your hands off!"

"I heard what you said, sweetheart. I was just hoping, for your sake, you wanted to rephrase that statement." His eyes darken as he pulls me to my feet and leads us up the stairs.

Why is he so mad?

"Ashley and I are just trying to have fun!" I protest.

He looks around the room before sighing. "I'll deal with her later. She should have never brought you here. Now go," He demands, waving his hand.

As we walk down the hall, I peer into an open VIP room and spot a sparkly red dress. *Yup, Ashley is safe…and she's on top of Ricky?* I quicken my steps, so Aiden will not see her, and step into the other VIP room. It looks nicer and bigger than the one before. A solitary black leather couch hugs the only pop of color in the room, a scarlet wall.

Aiden gestures for a nearby bouncer. His nameplate is blurry, but I think it says Max, who at this point, is three Max's.

"Don't allow anyone into this room," Aiden instructs.

"Of course, Boss." Max turns away and stands guard at the edge.

Aiden closes the thick fabric, hiding us from wandering gazes.

I get a little nervous as he stalks towards me. I've never seen him so angry before. I hear him mumbling something I can't decipher under his breath. It turns me on when he speaks Italian.

He runs his hand through his thick hair, a nervous habit. "I really thought you would listen to me and stay out of trouble, but here you are." He chuckles. "I'm just thankful you're at my club, of all the places."

Red flashes across my eyes. "Why do you care!" I shout in a drunken rage. "Go call Rebecca if I'm such a problem in your life!" I try and fail to not stumble over my words, but the alcohol slurs them.

He tilts his head to the side, studying me. He places a hand on his chin in thought and I watch as his muscles flex through the fabric of his suit.

"The girl from the lobby earlier."

"Yeah, her! She…she was supposed to stay the night with you." I stomp my feet, wobbling down onto the couch.

Aiden sits beside me and drags me onto his lap. Our bodies are so close I can feel the warmth from his skin. I beat down my need for him fiercely.

"I do…don't want to sit on you!" I pout, squirming on his lap.

"Fuck, baby. Don't move around too much or you'll make me hard."

I can't help but stare as he bites his bottom lip. *No, Emma! Control of yourself!* I cross my hands over my chest.

"That doesn't help," Aiden comments.

I look at him, confused.

"All you're doing is accentuating your cleavage."

His eyes trail down the same time as mine. He's right, they're practically falling out of my dress. I hastily pull the fabric up, before attempting to wiggle off him again. He holds my hips in place and thrusts up into me. I can feel his already hard length against my ass.

"I love this dress. I just wish it wasn't so tight. It shows too much." His voice is low as he runs his hand along the soft fabric. "From now on, you wear this only when you're out with me, understood?" he's completely ignoring why I'm upset.

I want to tell him, "That's why I bought it, idiot," but I have to get to the bottom of this Rebecca situation. "Explain yourself," I slur, feeling more and more drunk as the minutes roll by.

He lets out a long breath, mint invades my senses.

"First off," He holds up a finger, "I don't have to explain myself. The first thing you should have done was called me." He slides both hands up my thighs, causing the fabric of my dress to roll up slightly.

He keeps his eyes on mine. "Second, to be honest, I don't remember a Reba or whatever."

I snicker at the butchering of her name. But can I trust him?

"I don't believe you," I state quietly.

He holds my legs tighter. "You're mine as much as I'm yours. End of story." I try to ignore the warmth I feel in my heart at his words.

"But why would she say that?" I whine.

He shifts in the seat, running a large hand over his face. "I don't know. I'm assuming she knew you were in the lobby for me, and she was messing with your head. She's nothing to worry about, I promise you. No one is."

His words and tone are calm and sincere, and I believe him.

His smooth voice is replaced by a deep growl. "Now, let's talk about what the fuck you were doing grinding some guy? I should go out there and beat the fuck out of him in front of you, so you can see what happens when someone else touches you."

Despite his venomous tone, his hands are gentle as he plays with my loose curls, twirling them around his long fingers. I know he's a hot head, but I feel safe in his arms. He would never hurt me intentionally.

He leaves the room, returning moments later with a plate of food. "Eat," He demands, setting the plate in my lap and moves a glass of water closer to the edge of the table.

I happily grab the fries from the plate. "Why does this taste so good?" I look up with a smile.

Aiden stares at me intently, no trace of humor behind his jade eyes.

"Feel better?" He asks, once I'm done with the food. "More sober?"

I nod. I do feel so much better now that the alcohol is fading.

"Good. Now, how do you think I should deal with this?" He asks with a sly smirk.

"Forgive me because I thought you didn't want me?" I bat my lashes.

He laughs. "I will always want you Emma.

Seriously, I do." His words roll off his tongue like velvet. He waves a finger in thought. "But, regardless, actions have consequences, and I need you to be in order."

"Order?"

He nods, trailing his finger along my arm. "I have an urge to punish you."

"Punish me?"

"Mhmm, how should I go about this?" He asks himself, his hand gripping my thigh.

I swallow, excited by his words.

"Do you want to bend over my lap, Emma?"

———————

I stare, oddly excited about his request.

Without thinking, I lay myself over his lap, my eyes set on the black tile floors against Aiden's dress shoes. He lifts my dress, exposing my bare bottom to the cool air of the room. I look back to see him shaking his head in disapproval.

"No panties?" His voice rumbles with anger.

"I didn't want to wear them. The dress is too tight, and the lines show." I explain, hoping he didn't think I didn't wear any for another man.

He shakes his head and turns my head to face the floor. He rubs my bottom. "I should rip this tiny dress off your perfect skin and fuck you senseless to teach you a lesson."

"A lesson?" Again, with those words, lesson, and punish. I can't deny the fire they ignite inside of me.

"For disobeying me." His eyes darken, his touch

feather light against my bare bottom.

Biting my lip, I act on my liquid courage. "Punish me."

I feel a rush of air across my bottom before his hand lands firmly on my cheek. The sting makes me gasp. A tingle shoots straight to my clit. His warm hand ordering me into submission turns me on more than I have ever been. He brings out something in me. It feels natural to be laid over his lap like this, so much so that it worries me. *Is something wrong with me?*

"What I would give for you to be bouncing on my cock right now…" His voice is a soothing rumble.

His hand comes down on my bare cheeks, and by the third smack, I can't bear the pleasure that consumes my body. I wiggle, needing to relieve the tension and the throbbing ache inside me. I rock against his knee, moaning as I apply the right amount of pressure on my clit.

Aiden reaches between my legs and slides his fingers through my slit. They stay on my clit, circling and stroking it. "I'm making you wet." His tone is pleased. "You're too drunk for me to do anything sexual to you."

He pulls me flush against him, my trembling legs straddling him. The stinging sensation lingers as his fingers trail on my shoulders. I don't want it to go away, a reminder that his hands were on me. *What is wrong with me?*

"I want you."

He cups my chin, our lips so close I can smell his minty breath. "Too bad, sweetheart."

Playing this cat and mouse game doesn't help. I need him, crave him. Bringing my lips to his neck I plant kisses on his skin, gently rocking my body against him.

He grips my waist, halting my movements. "You're drunk, babe."

I lay my head against his chest, breathing deeply to calm myself. "I'm so sorry." I bite my lip, wanting to please him.

"You have to obey me." The word 'obey' rolls of his tongue in a sexual manner, overpowering my senses.

I continue to bite my lip, nervously.

"What's wrong?"

"I just…" I pause, trying to keep my words from slurring. His presence is intoxicating. "I like when you're like this."

He nods, not a hint of judgement in his tone. "You're discovering what you like, and I'm so fucking happy I have the honor of showing you everything." His fingers graze my bare shoulder. "But if you ever feel uncomfortable about anything, just let me know, okay?"

"Is something wrong with me for liking those things?"

A small laugh escapes his lips. "No, babe, nothing is wrong with you. I'm actually relieved you don't mind me being a little rough." He kisses my neck. "I want to throw you on the bed and have my way with you. I knew you would be submissive, but fuck, I'm so excited for when you're fully sober and I can do whatever I want to you." He growls into my ear.

I squeeze my legs together, hoping for some

relief.

He looks down at my shuffling. "Another thing." He tugs my legs apart. "There's no need for you to touch yourself." He bites his lip as his eyes trail up and down my body.

"Why?"

"You're mine…this cunt is mine." He stares into my eyes as he places his hand over it, covering me fully. "I can take care of you. I can make you feel things you never thought you could."

I shiver at his words, the fire burning deep inside me. He tilts his head, waiting for an answer. I want to turn him on. Maybe if I play into this fun side, he'll understand I'm sober now and we can mess around.

I straddle his waist as I play with his hair, peering at him with innocent eyes. "Yes, Mr. Scott."

I'm surprised by how natural my words sound. But my voice startles me the most, seductive and low. I can tell Aiden is surprised too as his breathing picks up.

"I've got to get you out of here. Let's get you home. We'll go find Ashley."

Remembering how indisposed Ashley is, I place a hand on his chest. "Wait." I don't know if he'll freak out about Ashley and Ricky. "I'll go grab her."

He tilts his head to the side. "You're not going anywhere." His words are final as he squeezes my hand before heading for the door.

"Please," I beg, stumbling slightly.

He raises a brow. "Are you worried about me catching her with Ricky?" He laughs. "I'm more perceptive than that. I already saw them as we walked up here."

"Are you mad at her?"

He laughs. "Why would I give a fuck? She's grown up and can do whatever she wants. Plus, I'm fucking her best friend so…"

I stop in my tracks. "I'm grown and I can't do whatever I want," I protest.

He lifts my face, so I'm forced to look into his eyes. "You're mine, princess. I don't give a fuck what anyone in the world does. As long as they aren't messing with you, it's none of my business." He wraps one hand protectively around my waist as we walk down the hall.

He tugs open the curtain to the other VIP room. "Drive her back to my place."

I hear Ashley scream and some shuffling. Aiden laughs as we head downstairs.

Aiden

I lift Emma into my arms. She's exhausted from the events of the day and I can't blame her. I make sure to hold her dress down. I can't believe she didn't wear any panties.

The thought infuriates me, but I can't help but imagine how easy it would've been to slip inside her earlier. It's too bad she drank tonight. I would never take advantage of her. Teasing is one thing, but anything more would be too much.

I gently place her in the Mercedes and buckle her in. I slide in quietly, pressing the ignition and hearing the twin turbo engine purr to life. She stirs but doesn't wake. I take a moment to take in her features; she looks so sweet and innocent, with her face smushed against the leather seat.

I'm thankful she's safe. I have to protect her from the horrors of the world. Even if I am one of them, I'm too selfish to stay away from her.

My mind wanders to what just happened. I had to restrain myself from taking her right there on the couch when she started grinding on my leg while I spanked her.

I don't know what this girl is doing to me. We were fooling around but I felt a primal urge to teach her a lesson. Any other girl, I would have just said fuck it and not dealt with the drama. But it's just different with Emma.

At the thought of her ass bouncing on my knee and the wetness I felt when I checked her pussy, the bulge in my pants grows. I need relief badly. I wish more than anything that none of this happened, that we were at home and she was sober so we could fuck.

At a red light, I peek over. The moon casts a faint glow on her tiny silhouette. One of her breasts hangs out from the thin fabric of her dress. That fucking dress. I rub myself through my pants, attempting to relieve some of my tension.

Unable to handle the throbbing, I unzip my pants and grasp my length, gently stroking it as I remember the way she grinded against me earlier. I want to hold her by her waist and slam her onto my cock while I revel in the feeling of her stretching around me. And since she was a bad girl and wore no panties, it would be easy to simply slide into her. I can't wait for tomorrow so I can do just that. I pump my cock to the thoughts of her.

Fuck, I'm driving down the road while doing this. Why couldn't I have waited until I got home and was in the safety of the bedroom or shower? What if she wakes up? Fuck it, she already knows she's mine and I'm hers. It's not like I'm doing anything directly to her.

I park the car in the lot. It's dark, but a street light surrounds her body with a warm glow. I pump harder and faster as I stare at her beautiful body imagining her plump lips sliding down my cock. Or the way her body responds so innocently to my touch, how she moans when I twirl her perfect nipples between my fingers. She's never been touched by a man before me, and that turns me on so fucking much. The pressure builds and I silently moan her name as I release into my hand.

Using a spare T-Shirt from the back to clean myself off, I fix her dress before carrying her inside, pulling down the thin fabric of her short dress to shield her from wandering eyes.

Tomorrow, she's in for it.

Eleven

I wake in Aiden's bed, tangled in his heavy comforter. I can't remember how I got here.

My head throbs from the fading light washing into the room, along with my hangover. My eyes finally adjust, and I see a glass of water and two Motrin on the nightstand. I groan as I take the medicine.

Why does my ass hurt?

Realization hits me, as everything that happened last night floods my hungover mind. I had fun when he showed up, but I feel ashamed for everything else. Not that I went to the club, but that I went out of spite, thinking he was supposed to be with Rebecca the night before.

I should have texted Aiden. Then I wouldn't have made a fool out of myself. But then we wouldn't have played around, and I wouldn't have discovered this new side of me.

Why did I like his hands on me in such a firm manner?

I stand sluggishly and stretch before grabbing my phone. My eyes widen when I see the time. Six p.m. I slept all day. Shit...I feel so guilty. I need to make it up to him, he needs to know how much I want him and no one else.

I use the restroom and wipe the sleep from my eyes. The reflection in the bathroom mirror makes me gasp. I'm wearing one of Aiden's button-ups. I wonder if he put it on me. Last night is a complete blur. When will he be home? I can text him but I'm not sure if I should.

I hurry and make myself looker better, sexier. I slap on some makeup before running a brush through my hair and tying it in a loose side braid. I slip on the lingerie Aiden bought before unbuttoning some buttons on his shirt to show off the bra. Once done, I wait patiently by the door.

The door clicks open minutes later and Aiden walks in. He rakes his eyes up and down my body slowly. "Fuck." I'm happy he's alone, I know he upped security and it would have been extremely embarrassing if he wasn't alone in the elevator.

Without another word, he drops his suit jacket and folders on the countertop before picking me up. I wrap my legs around him as he carries me into the room. He tosses me on the bed and hovers over me, trailing a long finger down my chest. In one motion, he unclasps the front buckle and yanks the fabric away, exposing my breast.

"You look so fucking good in my shirt." His voice is a low growl as his warm hands spread evenly over my breast.

I blush. "I... I missed you." I glance over at the windows. The view here is so beautiful, so romantic.

He curls a finger around my chin, forcing me to look at him. "I missed you too." His voice is velvet smooth as he trails kisses down my neck.

Shivers rake down my body as he fondles my breasts. He nudges one leg between my open legs, and I grind myself against him to relieve the pressure.

"Calm down, baby." He brings his fingers to my slit, gently rubbing it in circular motions. The sound of my wetness fills the room. "You've been sitting here thinking about me?" His hand caresses my center.

Nervous but excited, I nod. Running my hands through his styled hair, we collide. Our kiss is passionate, full of need.

"I own you." His breath hot and cool against my neck as he sucks on it, creating a hickey.

I rock against his hand, but he pulls it away when I'm on the brink of my release. His fingers dance up to my breast, he pinches my nipples eliciting a moan from my lips. Leaning his head down he brings his tongue to replace his fingers, his teeth gently pull on my erect nipples as I run my hands through his thick hair.

He moves between my legs and I feel how hard he is as he grinds against me, torturing me with his slow movements. I moan as he presses deeper into me. But to my dismay, he pulls away, leaving me withering beneath him.

I wish I was brave enough to tell him what I want, but I think he's doing this on purpose.

"You're so fucking perfect." He coos, gliding his hands over my body.

Anxiety washes over me as he kisses my stomach, going lower with each kiss. Eventually, he rips my panties off, grabs my legs and jerks me farther down the bed. My gasps turn into a moan as he buries his face between my thighs. His tongue expertly circles my clit, the feeling is so sensational I don't think I can take much more.

I tug on his hair and feel his groan rumbling against me. "I'm about…to…"

He pulls away right before I become putty under his hands…well, mouth.

"Stop teasing me!" I yell through a loud moan.

He slaps my ass, hard. When I look at him between my legs, I can tell his demeanor has changed into something more serious.

"I can't get the image of your ass grinding against that fucking dude out of my head." He hisses. "You're mine, Emma. No man will ever make you feel like I do."

He fucks me with his fingers fast and hard until I'm squirming with pleasure, whimpers pouring from my lips. He lays beside me, his body pressed against me. I can feel him against my leg. I want to say something, but I can't. I cling onto his body. I'm on the edge but I'm not sure if he will pull away again.

"Can I come now?" I pant, praying he will allow

me too. The anticipation of his permission turns me on even more.

"Yes, you may." He growls, thrusting more erratically but his movements are still precise.

I come with a scream moments later, but he continues his assault on my clit. My body trembles and jerks, overwhelmed by pleasure.

"I…I'm finished," I whisper through moans, trying to jerk away as the pleasure becomes too much.

His fingers never let up as his other hand pins my hip down. "You'll be finished when I say you are." He growls. I feel myself grow wetter at his words. "Now, tell me who owns this pussy?"

I moan. "You do, Aiden."

"Good girl." He slows his movements and pulls me upright, flush against his throbbing bulge. He grips my hips firmly as he moves my body roughly, making me grind against him. "Now, who owns you?"

I cum for the second time, screaming his name, which brings a smile to his face. I move to undo his pants, but he grabs my wrist.

"As much as I want to fuck your brains out, I'm still pretty pissed about last night."

I frown. "I really am sorry, but I've been waiting for you all day." Trailing a finger along his jawline, I plant a kiss on his lips.

He grabs my hips, and my stomach growls, causing his eyebrows to raise. "Did you eat today?"

I shake my head.

"Up, kitchen now," He orders, and I follow

reluctantly.

He pulls out a ton of options and I mindlessly pick through them. There's only one thing on my mind and it's not on this counter. I know I just came but I want him inside me, I need him.

I glance over at Aiden. I know this is a stupid thing to do but, "I guess if you don't want me, I can always go to a party and..." I don't finish my fib, surprised at my words as my cheeks redden.

Aiden stalks over to me, taking deep calculated breaths, before gently wrapping his hand around my throat. The throbbing between my legs grows and I squeeze my legs together. He's awakened my sexual desires in ways I never thought possible.

"The fuck you will," He growls. "Bend over that fucking table."

***

I obey his request.

His hands are tight around my waist as he grinds against me. I wiggle my ass against his length, letting him know how much I want him in me. I hear a zipper flying down, and a wrapper being ripped open, before he rams into me from behind. I let out a moan as he stretches me almost uncomfortably. He grips my braid as he pumps in and out of me at a steady, rhythmic pace.

"You fucking love this, don't you?" He growls, slapping my ass.

I try to nod my head but his grip on my hair is too tight, causing twinges of pain which in turn causes the pleasure to override my senses.

"You're such a good girl for me. Fuck."

His words unravel me.

"You're mine." Aiden pounds harder into me. His hands caress me from behind, his gentle touches make me shiver as he slides his hand down my spine. "So fucking soft." He tells me, bringing his mouth to kiss my shoulder. Reaching around, he fondles my breast. Kneading and pulling on my nipples. His body shudders as I feel him filling the condom with hot liquid.

He grabs my waist and sits me on the table, before going to toss the spent condom. He cups my face and plants a soft kiss on my lips, before leaning his forehead against mine as our breathing calms.

"What are you doing to me?"

"I'm not doing anything." I giggle.

He throws on a pair of gray drawstring pants, discarding his work clothes. I stare, taking in how his tan skin looks against the black ink that adorns his perfect body. The way his messy black hair has fallen over his emerald eyes makes me melt, and his half-smile causes my stomach to flutter. I wonder if I'm falling head over heels for this man.

Needing a distraction, I reach my hands up and tickle him.

He jerks, looking at me in surprise before attacking me. "Oh, you messed up now, angel."

He throws me over his shoulder, his hands on my sides as he tickles me. I laugh obnoxiously, loving this playful side of him. He's normally so serious, I have a feeling he hardly ever loosens up.

Aiden throws me on the couch, climbing on top of me and tickling me until I scream from laughter. I let out an extremely embarrassing snort, which causes him to double over in laughter.

"You sounded like a little pig." He laughs.

I blush. "Shut up."

But I don't want him too, not wanting this moment to end.

But alas…all good things always come to an end.

I should have known better. I should have tried to stay in that moment a little longer before disaster struck.

I should have ran.

But I didn't.

Twelve

Complete darkness surrounds me. The shuffling of feet and the ice-cold concrete floor beneath me are the only signs that I'm not dreaming. But I still don't know where I am. Fear I've never experienced envelops me as I tremble against the cold ground.

A voice speaks up, heavily accented. "Aiden Scott will be here shortly; I don't doubt that he has trackers on them." I'm breathing heavily, what kind of business is Aiden into? What do these men want with us?

It feels as though hours have passed before someone finally rips the blindfold off, revealing a dark, damp room. I squint my eyes, seeing only concrete walls. A slight movement jolts me, and I turn but I'm bound tight. My eyes adjust to the dim lighting and, to my horror, unfamiliar male faces dot the room. Staring at me, their guns slack.

I tuck my legs in against my stomach. Trying frantically to remember the things my dad told me about staying calm in dangerous situations. That's when I notice my back is pressing against something warm that's shaking. A sob penetrates the fear that has settled around me. Ashley.

"It will be okay," I whisper through a dry mouth, my trembling voice loud in the tiny, sparse room.

I flinch as a man with a greasy ponytail walks up. His face is set in an ugly scowl as he yells in another language. Unable to move away, I brace myself as his hand lifts and hits me squarely across the cheek. My head snaps to the side from the force of his hand. I scream as the sharp crack rings through the room. I feel something wet trickling down my chin. He drew blood. I bite back a sob as my cheek throbs painfully.

I shrink into myself, putting my head down. That's when I realize my state of undress. I'm only in my bra and panties. A wave of nausea washes over me, knowing that these men had stripped me down while I was unconscious and vulnerable. I shiver as fear floods me. Who knows what else they might have done to us.

I squeeze my eyes shut, wanting to block out the horror.

Out of sight, out of mind, right? Not.

Ashley and I had just finished shopping that morning and were heading to the parking lot where our driver was waiting for us. Thinking back on the oddly quiet lot and the echo of our footsteps, I should have known better. Dad always said to have your keys out and tucked between your knuckles like a weapon. I didn't know anything would happen, and I wasn't prepared.

As we approached the car, a dark spot pooling on the pavement caught my eye. Stepping closer, I rounded the car to examine it and gasped at the gruesome sight. I vaguely heard Ashley let out a chilling scream. I will never forget those cold, lifeless eyes of Maxon staring up at me from where he lay splayed on the ground.

I swallow as I recall the bullet wound in the middle of his forehead, still oozing blood and other yucky stuff. Guilt overwhelms me. He's a nice guy, although a little serious. And he'll still be alive, if not for us.

I remember spinning around when I heard doors opening. My face paled when four mean-looking men jumped out of a black suburban. Shouting for Ashley to run, I moved to do so as well. But a large hand yanked my arm back roughly before a cloth was placed over my mouth and nose. The last thing I remember was a slightly sweet smell and a sinister laugh before the world around me went dark.

I send a prayer up to Heaven.

Aiden, please come get me soon.

I jerk as something cold and hard presses roughly against my temple, my eyes flying open. *A gun*, my mind helpfully offers.

"Look at me!" Ponytail demands in a heavily accented voice.

"Leave her alone you fucking greaseball!" Ashley screams, her cries echo through the room. He removes the gun from my temple, bringing it in front of her. Fear courses through me, is he about to hurt her?

The sound of metal hitting bone makes me cry out, "Are you okay?" I cry, terrified for her.

"Yes." She says, her head rolling back slightly. A tear rolls down my cheek as I shrink back into Ashley, whose cries have increased in volume.

I'm going to die.

Oh my God, I'm going to die.

Aiden

I'm back at Corvallis, grabbing some of Emma's things.

Since Ashley is staying with Ricky, there's no fucking way in hell I'm allowing my girl to stay at this house alone. There's no need for her to be here anyway since school is out. She tried to come with me, but I sent her shopping instead.

I know Emma loves the little place, but it's garbage. I'm not against small homes; they can be quaint and cozy, if done right, but this place is a pit.

I can read people well, I've always been able to. Emma is the first girl I've come across in my life that is truly pure and good. But the first time I laid with her in her room, as I twirled her hair while she slept, her head pillowed on my chest and her sleepy breaths resonating in my ears, my eyes wandered to the speckled ceiling of her bedroom and I noted a hole in the drywall. My eyes trailed down to the bucket I hadn't noticed that collected water on the floor.

That, and the many other things wrong with the house made the decision for me. I curse my piece of shit father for not being around for Ashley. The fact that he's not in her life and wasn't there to help her when she chose to rent instead of living on campus infuriates me and smothers me in guilt, I should have been there to help her... I am now. And it was in that moment I knew I wanted the girls out of the house.

I had my realtor greenlight my penthouse, no matter the cost. It costed an extra ten thousand to get it done so quickly, but I'm willing to pay whatever for her to live somewhere that didn't affect her health. Ashley too.

I need to get the girls out of there. I have fixed their clogged sink four times in a week. I wish Ashley had talked to me, but it's my fault. I need to be a better brother.
So busy and wrapped up in my career, I put her – my only real family – on the sidelines. But not anymore. I'm going to set the girls up.

The moving company is coming by today.

I have not told the girls yet. Hopefully, they aren't too pissed.

I place Emma's neatly folded clothes into her new Tiffany & Co. suitcase my personal assistant, Carmello, got. I know she'll adore the luggage, seeing as her room is in Tiffany blue, before turning it away with a shy smile, embarrassed about me spending money on her. When that happens, I'll ease her suffering by telling her I already had it in my closet.

I'm sure I'll look funny carting around such a feminine suitcase.

But fuck it, what my girl likes is what she'll get.

I grab some dresses I know she'll look adorable in from her closet, relieved to find them modest looking. The thought of her parading around town, showing too much skin makes me seriously mental, though I'm sure she'll look sexy as fuck in anything. Men will turn their heads no matter what she's wearing. She doesn't need to help the process.

I grab her things and a small vase from the bathroom. I noticed the vase always sat empty and I offered to get her a new one. I mean, it couldn't fit more than one single flower. She declined. Maybe I'll start bringing flowers to the apartment.

Passing by Ashley's room reminds me of the talk I had with her about taking Emma to the club. She wasn't happy, but eventually gave in when I stood my ground. She said Emma's changing me.

Fuck she is. I won't change for anything.

My phone buzzes incessantly in my pocket as I lock up. I fumble with the luggage and keys, cursing myself for not hiring someone to do this. I didn't want a mover touching her panties and things. They can get everything else. I set the luggage in the truck of the car and pull out my phone.

Ricky's name flashes on the screen.

Heavy breathing and cuss words echo from the other end of the line.

My body stiffens.

"They took them. The fucking Matarazzo's took the girls."

Tunnel vision.

Panic.

Seething fucking rage.

I curse myself for lying to her about what I do for a living.

I'm going to fucking kill them for even thinking about harming my little sister. I'm going to torture them until they beg for absolute mercy for even looking at my girl.

Another call comes through, breaking me from my trance as I speed down the freeway. Clicking the button on the dash, the voice of the man I'm about to kill bleeds through the speakers of my Mercedes.

"Hello, Mr. Scott." A familiar accented voice sounds on the other end.

Vinny Matarazzo.

Pure rage lines my tone. "Tell me where the fuck they are."

My hands grip the steering wheel tightly as I head

towards the city, going at least a hundred miles an hour.

"Tsk, tsk. I call the shots, understand?"

His arrogance would make me laugh if I wasn't so enraged and in fear for my girl and Ash. I've never felt this before. This fear coursing through my veins.

"Get to the fucking point, Vinny," I spit out, imagining my hands around his neck, watching the life drain from his pointless existence.

"I'll call you with the details later."

And the line goes dead.

A maniacal laugh escapes my clenched teeth. I thank God I have a tracker on Em. I know it's a little crazy, but her safety is the absolute most important thing to me. After the stunt they pulled with the club, ditching my driver, I'm not taking any chances.

Picking Ricky up, we hightail to where her locator last pinged. An industrial part of town. Nightfall creeps on us and we use it to our advantage. Parking a block away, we prowl towards the vast number of warehouses, slowing as we try and decide which one they might be in.

A muffled scream is a giveaway, and the familiar tone behind it makes my body shake with rage.

"I'm going to fucking kill everyone in that building." I whisper to Ricky as we walk closer. Trying to keep a low profile as we size up the building. It's not a huge place but big enough to hold a lot of men. But there is no time for reconnaissance, we have to make our move now.

I turn to Ricky, letting every ounce of authority creep into my words. If he fucks this up...I can't even think of that. "You get Ashley. I'll get Emma. Clean break. If we can't get them out for any reason, I kill every last one of them, and you shield the girls, understand?"

He nods, cocking his gun.

I double check the gun tucked into my waistband. "Under no circumstance do you save me if it puts them in danger."

Creeping towards a large metal sliding door, I know whoever is inside will be alerted of our presence the moment I pull it open, but we have no other choice. I may not be thinking clearly, but I know I have to get them out of there. Carefully, I pull open the door. Ricky follows close behind as we walk inside the cool warehouse. I keep my gun drawn as my eyes adjust to our new surroundings.

The muffled sounds become clearer as we round a narrow hallway. I peek my head around the side of a concrete wall, trying to decipher how many men we're up against.

Rage burns through my veins at the sight of Ash and Emma tied up, back to back, in just their underwear. These men have sealed their fates. I'm going to kill everyone involved. Their family, their friends. Fuck, even their distant cousins.

I hold seven fingers up to Ricky before walking in the open area. They should have had more men throughout the warehouse if they wanted to get away with whatever this is.

Vinny looks in my direction, unsurprised, a cocky grin on his face. He must think his six men dotted around the room are more than enough to stop me.

Not a chance.

"Took you long enough." Vinny twirls a sharp knife as he steps closer to Emma. Her eyes light up when she sees me, as if I'm her hero. She's bolted to the fucking ground because of me, how can she look at me like that? Then, as if realization slaps her in the face she screams, "It's a trap! They lured you here!" The dried blood on her face makes my jaw clench.

I inch forward, halting when he brings the knife to her throat.

"You can have anything you want. Name it. Just let the girls go."

He laughs sinisterly.

I tighten my hand around the gun.

"You can't give me back my daughter," He growls. The dull fluorescent light accents the gleam of his knife.

He's right. I can give him money and power, practically anything in the world. But I can't bring back the dead. What happened was never my fault, but I should never have gotten involved with the Mafia. Back then, I had nothing to lose.

Things are different; I'm not the same man. I have everything to lose now. Vinny's a desperate man, but what he doesn't understand is what he's holding beneath that sharp blade. My world.

Standing straight, I aim the barrel at his chest. "That wasn't my doing." I spit.

There's no point trying to reason with him.

"Eye for an eye. Can't find the men who did it...yet. She'll do for now." He shrugs, running the dull side of the knife against her soft shoulder. She tries to be strong, but I can see her body shaking violently.

My finger lightly squeezes the trigger. The only thing stopping me is the fear of him accidentally cutting her, even the slightest nick on her skin won't be tolerated.

"Put the gun down, or this pretty one gets a gash on her precious face." His voice is devoid of any emotion. He sounds...bored.

I don't obey. The second I do, I'll be a target for his men. If I die, who will keep the girls safe?

"Wrong choice." He sneers, lightly skimming her cheek with the blade.

I growl lowly as she cries out, a line of blood dripping down her face.

"See, Aiden." He drawls, his voice laced with humor. "I have your *sorella* and your *piccolo*. I want to keep them. They're just so...obedient when they're passed out." He chuckles.

As he laughs, hatred fuels me. He has to die.

"If you fucking touched either one of them, I swear to God." I choke.

The odds are against us, I know they are. But Emma shouldn't have to see me this way, and she definitely shouldn't see what I'm about to do. If I die, it will only be after I squeeze the life out of every man in this fucked up warehouse.

I stare at Emma's beautifully terrified face, trying to memorize her every feature. I mask the anger in my voice, using that gentle tone I always use with her, not wanting her to remember my last words as mean or hateful. "Close your eyes."

I thank God she listens, because the second her eyes close, I pull the trigger. A loud bang sounds and a bullet pierces dead between Vinny's eyes. Bullets fly, ricocheting in every direction.

Four men left.

I shield Emma with my body, she cries out for me, but I can't turn for even a second. Ricky does the same for Ashley.

Only three men left.

Ricky wails in agony.

I turn to see him bent over, a bullet wound to his leg. Ashley is fighting against her chains to be by his side.

"I'm fine." He growls, straightening before pulling the trigger.

One to go.

Lucio Matarazzo, Vinny's brother. His eyes burn with unadulterated rage as he glances at Vinny. Blood pools beneath his head, and the sight makes me laugh.

I want Lucio to suffer, the others died too quickly for my liking. I shoot his hand and his gun clatters to the ground as he shouts. I throw my head back, unable to control my dark laughter at the sight of his world falling apart.

Caught in my quest for vengeance, I fail to notice the gun hidden in his waistband until I hear a loud bang and a burning pain sears my chest as the bullet slices through me. Emma's piercing scream rings in my ears as I look down and see red seeping through my white T-shirt at an alarmingly fast rate.

I curse myself for not wearing black. The girls shouldn't have to see this.

I grunt as the pain grows. I press down on the wound, trying to stem the blood. Luckily, I hear Lucio's gun jamming. Feeling faint, I do the only good thing I've ever done in my life. I empty my magazine into Lucio's chest as my sight blurs and I feel my body going slack.

My sister's safe. My girl, my beautiful girl, is safe.

I will gladly bleed out on the cold concrete if it means she will not endure another scratch.

Fourteen

P ain. The overwhelming agony when you lose someone you love is unbearable, unthinkable. No words can express the emotions when your heart is ripped from your chest and stepped on. When a life is cut too short.

Pain, they say, gets better with time. Thank God I won't have to find out.

Thank God Aiden is okay.

I watch his still body on the hospital bed, connected to beeping machines, with heavy eyes. Their rhythmic beeps echo inside my head as I wait for him to open his eyes. Needles are sunk into his skin and a bandage covers his entire chest.

I hold my breath when I hear a groan.

"Did they touch you?" are the first words out of his lips.

I laugh. I know I shouldn't, but my heart is filled with so much joy. A weight has been lifted from my chest.

"No." I make my way to his bedside, running my fingers through his black hair.

"Don't lie." He croaks, pushing himself up stubbornly.

I place a gentle hand on his shoulder, pushing lightly to get him to lie back down. He's been unconscious for three days, massive blood loss and damage to his head will do that. He fell on the hard concrete upon blacking out, it broke my heart that I couldn't reach him as I fought against my restraints.

He tilts his head, taking in the bandage on his chest, and ignores it. "Please, tell me." His fingers circle the healing scab on my cheek, like it's something serious.

I bite my lips, embarrassed. I shake my head. "They didn't. Ashley and I, we're kind of in sync." I gesture to my abdomen.

He shoots me a confused look.

I sigh. "I started my period that morning, so did she..." I blush.

He smiles, gesturing for me to continue.

"We...we both had tampons in. Still intact." I put my hands in front of me.

"Thank God." He wraps a heavy arm around my waist and pulls me onto the bed, laying me across his chest.

I gasp, yanking myself away. "Are you crazy?" I exclaim, moving to check his bandage. "I could've squished you and opened your stitches!"

He rolls his eyes. "Oh, baby, you can't even squish a fly." He pins me with puppy eyes, his voice soft and warm. "Please come here."

I carefully pillow my head on his chest, sighing as he plays with my hair.

Aiden wasn't too surprised when the doctor came by to explain what happened the past three days and how lucky he was to be alive. The bullet went through and through, and he passed out from blood loss. He even had stitches on his head from when he hit the concrete. What surprised me most was when the doctor accepted a wad of cash from a guard to keep quiet about everything.

He looks so broken lying on that hospital bed, I want to wrap his massive frame in my small arms and hold him. Thankfully they'll discharge him in a few days after monitoring the swelling in his brain.

"We need to talk about what's going on though," I hedge, feigning a calm expression.

I heard the men inside the warehouse. I know Aiden is doing some shady business. I trust him to keep me safe, but do I want that for the rest of my life? Maybe it's not as serious as it sounds. Aiden's a good guy. It probably is a misunderstanding.

He rubs his face. "I know, Em." He sighs. "It's a long story. Maybe when we get home?"

My heart flutters when he calls it home, our home.

Which reminds me… "So, I went home to change and found all of mine and Ashley's stuff in your living room?"

A half-smile creeps up his face. "You're going to kill me."

I nod, eyeing him warily. *What did he do?*

"Your rental is in Ashley's name. I kind of took the paperwork and broke the contract."

"You what?" I push myself up and glare down at him. But I can't stay mad with him looking so broken.

He shrugs. "You live in a shithole, Em. I'm not going to allow it."

"I think that's my decision," I point out.

He shakes his head. "You would never do that to your mom. I know you're both going broke. It's only a matter of time." His eyes plead with me to understand.

I take a deep breath. "Where are you moving us?"

"Well, I had this whole plan." He laughs a humorless laugh. "I had some houses for the both of you to look at with a realtor once you finished shopping that day. You never got the chance." He looks down.

I cup his cheek. "Okay, so explain why we never got the chance."

I can't be upset with him about the house thing, it isn't just me living there...it's his sister too. When he's less bandaged, I'll talk to him about it.

"I made a bad business choice." His voice is gruff and thick. "I was in college, building my business. How do you think I got all this at such a young age? Definitely not from following the rules." A small, deep laugh escapes his perfect lips.

He twirls my hair as I sit next to him, my fears

becoming a reality. *Who is he?*

"I'm an investor. I didn't lie about that." He sighs. "I met a CEO of a large investment company, who saw that I could hold my own. He offered me a proposition. Take on the 'criminal' clients; Mafia, organized crime, that sort of thing." He speaks nonchalantly.

"Why?"

He shrugs. "I wanted to be something. I have a piece of shit father, who's no help in my life. I did everything on my own, I had no privileges. I needed to be something more, so I thought, why not?" His eyes pierce mine. "I didn't have anything to lose...until you."

My voice trembles as I speak. "Will they come after you again?"

He shakes his head. "No, I'm hiring security detail for you and Ash. I'm also moving our stuff to another location. Don't worry, it'll still have pretty views." He smiles.

"I don't want this life anymore. What kind of castle do I have if the foundation is cracked and the throne is made of glass with nowhere for you to sit?"

His words warm me, but I can't shake my fear. Being kidnapped is traumatizing and I'm terrified it will happen again. I've seen too much loss in my life, between my father being taken from us so suddenly to what I've just experienced... It's too much.

After checking with the doctor five times to make sure Aiden will be okay, I hesitantly creep out of the room. I look back at his sleeping frame, remembering the feel of his hair as I stroke him to sleep before tearing my eyes away.

I almost turned around when I got to the lobby, almost.

I squint at the bright sun, lost in thought. Aiden's left me homeless, but there's still Mom's. I get his sentiment of wanting to stash us somewhere nicer and safer. It's sweet. How could he have foretold the events that happened?

I look down at my hands, still shaking from fear before lifting one to hail a taxi. I slip my phone out of the cracked window halfway towards Aiden's building. Those men had us for too long, and I can't risk them tracking me.

I keep a straight face as I speak with the security, telling him I'm getting a shower before taking some things back to the hospital, before stepping onto the elevator. I hesitantly walk into our room, his room, and begin to pack. There's no way I can get my furniture and things from where the movers dropped it off, but I guess I could get my own moving company.

I probably won't be doing another semester at college anyways since Mom is closing her shop. My heart breaks for her. Maybe I can get a job baking somewhere and help her with the bills.

My eyes landed on Aiden's gift. I thought it funny when Aiden claimed he already had the Tiffany blue suitcase. I knew he got it for me as it's my favorite color. But I can't take it with me; I settle for one of his shirts instead.

I bury my face in the black fabric, inhaling the intoxicating scent that is Aiden. Mint and leather, with a hint of smoke. A tear falls as I place the trunk on the bed before stuffing my belongings in a trash bag.

I thank God my car is parked at the penthouse.

"Hello baby." I pat the hood of my Altima and climb in. I wonder if Aiden has woken up and realized I'm gone.

First stop, gas station and a burner phone.

I need to know if Aiden and Ashley are okay. I know it's selfish to leave, then check up on him. But I care about him, more than myself. Which is why I can't let him chase me around, protecting me. He had a life before me.

I know he cares, but at what cost if I'm a burden in his life?

He said he wants to get his life together; I don't want to hinder his progress. Hiring security to watch after me will just make him worry about me instead of focusing on himself.

After what seems like days, I pull into the lot of Mom's flower shop at three in the afternoon. My breath hitches in my throat when I see every single parking spot is claimed. It looks like everyone in town is here. I had hoped no one was around so I can cry on my mom's shoulder.

I squeeze my Altima into a tight spot and head for

the front door, passing rose bushes and hundreds of colorful flowers. I always love coming here. The fact that she's losing the place breaks my heart. The old brass bell rings as I step in.

I watch as Mom turns towards the door, ready to give her usual "Welcome to The Flower Patch!" catchphrase.

Upon seeing me, she squeals with delight and barrels towards me. She wraps me in a tight hug I didn't know I needed. One of her famous Pamela Banks hugs. Her freshly highlighted hair masks my face as she clings tightly to me. She looks good, well-rested and happy.

Too many people are dotted throughout the place for me to cry and I hold it in, as she pulls back.

She looks me over, a slight frown taking shape on her round face. "Oh, honey. What happened?"

Her concerned voice unravels me. I'm lucky the shop is completely packed, noisy enough to muffle my sniffles. Kids laughing and the pitter-patter of their shoes against the hard floors as they run around. Grandparents fighting over which flower to plant in their yard, and finally...the clicking of my mother's impatient shoe.

I stall. "I'm fine, Mom. What's happening here?" I look around with wide eyes, gesturing to everyone.

She grabs my hand, leading me to the garden at the back of the shop. I smile as we pass the wall of yellow roses. "Oh honey, it's wonderful! I had an investor come in. He wanted to support hometown businesses." She claps her hands together.

Noting that no one is around, I can feel the tears

brewing again. I'm happy for her, but I feel so broken. I force a smile, but I know it's only a matter of time.

"We have enough to keep the shop open for another twenty years!"

The overwhelming relief of not having to worry about Mom mixed with the utter heartbreak of leaving Aiden overwhelms me, and I envelope her in a hug and burst into tears. Sobbing uncontrollably.

Minutes pass before she pulls back and studies me. "I know you're happy for me, but those are tears of sadness too. I'm your mother, I can tell these things." She gives me the look.

I nod once.

"Come!" She leads me inside. "I'll get one of the girls to run the shop for today. We can head home. I drove the work van here so we can take your car."

Relief floods me as the familiarity of my childhood home surrounds me.

The scent of cinnamon and apple wafts through the air. Our home smells like fall all year round, and I love it. Baby pictures of me lining the hallways make me smile, but it's the golden lab that is currently barreling towards me that warms my heart.

"Rex!" I exclaim in delight, falling to the ground from his weight as he jumps on me. "Who's a good boy?" I hug his soft golden body as he wiggles underneath me, his tail wagging hard. I missed him.

My mom laughs before she helps me up and

guides me to the kitchen table, the place where we have all our important discussions.

I tell her everything.

Well, not everything, but the gist of it. That I met a guy and I really liked him, but something happened. She hounds me, wondering if it's his fault, but I assure her that it isn't. I just want to come home and relax.

She's quiet as we sit at our old kitchen table. Scratch marks from years of use make me smile. She places her hand on mine and changes the subject, for that I'm grateful.

"What do you want for dinner? Absolutely anything. You name it, I'll make it."

"Umm, roast? And maybe apple pie?" I look at her hopefully.

I throw on a pair of slippers and go to grab the mail for Mom the next morning, Rex trotting along beside me. He's been following me everywhere. I think he knows that I've broken my own heart.

I see Caleb across the street. The boy who broke my heart in high school.

I stare as he washes his white truck in his driveway. The same truck he kissed the head cheerleader in, while we were dating. Why was I so caught up with him back then? That slight pain is nothing compared to the breaking of my heart when I left Aiden behind.

What if I made a mistake?
What if he's the one?

Aiden

When you find the one, you'll know.
       I know it.
       She knows it.
    Fuck. Everyone knows it.
    And yet, she left me.
    I don't blame her though. I quite literally put her life in danger. But I'll be damned if I let something as miniscule as the fear of the Mafia separate us. We're bigger than that. We're destined for something greater.
       I'd let her live without me, if I were a better man.
       But I'm not, and she's mine. It's all very simple, really.
       I'll get her back. I'll find her.

It won't be hard.

Ashley tried to keep it from me, but after I asked her fifty times, she broke. I found out Emma's been calling every few hours, wondering if I'm okay.

She's too precious.

I know she's safe. I only bothered Ash because I wanted to know if Emma contacted her. Em had a security detail on her since she left the hospital. Luckily, I told Ricky of my plans to have my best detail on the girls at all times before I got shot. I wanted them to follow her at every turn, and that's what they've done.

I'm upset that she left her stuff behind. I enjoy her having nice things. Her phone is the worst though, smashed on the side of the road. I hate having to check in with the security personnel to get an update on her. My clever girl threw it out in case the guys that took her had implanted a tracking device.

The hospital wanted to hold me longer but fuck that. Ricky was cleared the day after we were brought in and he's been taking care of Ash.

I want my girl, she's the one that can heal me. A bullet hurts less than her leaving. But again, I can't blame her. I need to prove to her that I can protect her. I'll let her breathe for a couple of days before coming for her.

I throw my hoodie in the backseat of my car, knowing she likes to sleep in it. I also sent her a gift, to let her know I am thinking of her.

I hope she likes it.

Sixteen

I pull on a light blue dress I had stuffed in the back of my closet and head to visit Dad. I stop by Mom's shop to grab a dozen yellow roses. It's a ten-minute drive and I'm so nervous the entire way. I already know I'm going to tell him everything. He always listens.

I gently place the flowers on the lush green grass at the bottom of his tombstone. I shed a million tears as I hug the cool marble slab. Yellow roses are what he bought for her every Friday when he got off of work.

She'll check him out and blush, asking, "For someone special?"

And he'll always respond with, "Only the most beautiful girl in the world."

He'll set them in a vase once she got home without fail, and he'll always take out one solitary rose for me and place it in a small vase.

They did this for twenty years.

I still have my vase, but it's been empty since he was murdered.

While I play with my solitary rose, gently plucking the yellow petals off in a childish game of 'He loves me, he loves me not', I tell him all about Aiden and what happened. I pray for him to show me a sign of what to do. I know he wouldn't want this life for me.

Dad was a lead detective. The fact that Aiden's tied up with criminals would be a problem, but I don't think he'd hate Aiden. He'd hate what he got himself into, but Dad was an understanding man. He'll get that Aiden's just trying his best to build a life for himself with the shitty hands he was dealt.

I've never told anyone about Dad. Ashley knows he isn't with us anymore, but she doesn't know what happened on that cold winter's night. I just can't bring myself to talk about what happened to him. I know I should, but it breaks me to pieces every time.

I place my hand on his tombstone, blowing him a kiss. "I love you, Dad. So much."

It's three when I pull into the driveway, deciding to check the mail.

It wasn't a good idea.

A familiar voice shouts my name as I close the lid. My eyes roll dramatically into the back of my head as Caleb makes his way over to me.

"Em! I didn't know you were home." He smiles, pulling his blonde hair out of his face.

I stare, willing myself to be cordial even though I want to punch him in the nose. Our families grew up together, so I don't want to be rude.

I fake a smile. "Hey."

I manage not to contort my face with the simple greeting. *Go, Emma.*

I'm not jaded about what he did, but how he did it. He told me he was too busy at the tackle shop to hang out on my birthday. So you can imagine my surprise when I caught the rudest girl in school straddling him in his truck, her tongue down his throat, a few hours later at a bonfire.

I've gotten over it, but I can't stand a cheater.

He steps in front of me, blocking my path to freedom, as I turn on my heel to walk away. This time, I visibly rolled my eyes.

"What's up, Caleb?" I ask in a disinterested voice.

"Just curious what you're doing back. I thought you had a place at college now?" He smiles.

I want to tell him how stupid he looks but I bite my lip instead. *It's summer, you idiot.*

"Ah, I see you still have the habit of biting your lip." He chuckles and crosses his arms.

I can tell he's flexing his muscles on purpose. Aiden would crush him like a bug. I take my lip out from between my teeth and change the subject. "How's your mom?"

"She's great! She'd actually love to see you. Want to come over for dinner tomorrow? You and Mrs. Banks."

I try to think of the best excuse I can but I'm coming up short. Besides, he'll just ask Mom if I say no, and everyone knows Pamela Banks would never turn down a dinner invite because it's rude.

I never told Mom Caleb and I dated. She always thought we were best friends. That way, he could come over and stay however late he wanted. It's not like we ever did anything crazy; I kissed him but that's it. Now I wish I had told her.

I hesitate for a moment before giving in, not figuring a way out. "Sure."

He flashes me one victory smile. "See you later."

I head inside, climb into my pajamas and sink into the warm bed. Speaking to Dad takes a load off me. I know he hears me; I just wish he was still here. It's easy to pretend he's here with Mom while I'm away at college, their laughter filling the house. But now, it feels empty. Mom tries her best, but we'll always be a puzzle with a hundred missing pieces without him.

My heart aches for Aiden, but I can't shake the nightmares. I've woken up screaming multiple times. Luckily, Mom believes me when I tell her it's PTSD. I hate using Dad's death as an excuse, but telling her the truth, that I was kidnapped, would break her. She's always been so supportive of my decisions; I don't want her to be paranoid.

A light knock on the front door prompts me to crawl out of bed. Mom's at work and my heart pounds with anticipation that it may possibly be Aiden.

It isn't.

Instead, a small Tiffany blue box sits on the front porch with a note attached.

You're still mine as much as I'm still yours. Wear this so everyone else knows it too.

Aiden's handwriting. I can't help my smile.

I know that he knows where I am. It's hard to not miss the black glossy escalade parked out front since I arrived. I didn't have my ID on me when I was taken so I know they don't know my address, and Ashley told them my name was Claire. But the extra security makes me feel better. Like Aiden is here himself, protecting me.

Gift in hand, I smile brightly at the car parked down the street and return inside. I carefully open the Tiffany box, too cute to tear into and ruin. I open the jewelry box and gasp when I see the beautiful necklace.

A delicate rose gold padlock is attached to a thin rose gold chain. The lock is closed, and the word 'Aiden' is embedded into the gold across the front. I put it on and admire how it looks against my skin. It's small and subtle. Just perfect.

I resist the urge to call him, to tell him how much I loved it. I'm sticking firm to my decision. I will not be a burden in his life.

Mom arrives home after a busy day at work, her

dark hair pulled back haphazardly. She looks exhausted.

The countertops are lined with macaroons and cupcakes after I spend the day baking to keep myself busy.

"Looks like we're having sweets for dinner." Mom laughs as she examines the treats dotting every inch of her kitchen, before picking up a macaroon and happily biting into it.

"Wow, Emma! These are deli–"

A loud knock on the door cuts her off and she makes her way back to the door. I hear it creak open before she speaks again, her voice is full of surprise.

"Mr. Scott?"

That name. Could It be?

My brain tells my feet to slow, but they don't listen. I glide out of the kitchen and into the hallway. That's when I see him standing in the doorway, leaning against the frame. He looks unusually casual in his black shirt and dark jeans, but still heavenly. His eyes are pleading as he looks between Mom and I.

He's here.

...I never showed Mom a picture of him, let alone told her his name. Definitely not his last name. So how does she know?

His deep velvet voice fills the house. "I'm sorry, Miss. Banks. I need to have a talk with your daughter."

He walks right past her and straight for me. Mom's face is twisted in confusion, as is mine, as he wraps me in a tight hug.

He buries his face in my hair. His chest rises and

falls as he breathes me in. "I missed you, baby. So much."

His strong arms envelope me, and I can't help but wrap mine around his neck.

I can't think straight. He smells too good. The familiar scent of my childhood home, cinnamon and apples, is replaced with another aroma. Mint and smoke, my other version of home.

My resolve falters and I squeeze his waist, he winces slightly, and I'm reminded of his wound. "Sorry." I whisper, my voice cracking.

I pull back and study his face, his features a mixture of relief with a hint of anger. His eyes pan down to my chest where his necklace lays. His uneven smile makes me melt.

I ask the one question that keeps running through my mind. "How do you know my mom?"

Mom walks up and smiles at Aiden, answering my question. "Honey, this is the man I was telling you about. The investor."

He places his hand on the small of my back.

"Well, this is the guy I was telling you about." I shoot him a curious glance.

He gives away nothing. His face is stone.

My mom pats his shoulder. "Now I see why you're so invested in a small business from a town you're not even from." She laughs, gesturing for us to sit.

She brews a pot of coffee and brings us each a mug before taking her spot at the table. Aiden is next to me and Mom across.

"So, Mr. Scott…"

He politely stops her with a smile. "Please, just Aiden."

"Aiden." She sits a little straighter. "What's going on here?" She looks between us and I wait for him to speak up. Thankfully, he does.

"Emma and I are together."

The way he says it sends shivers down my body. A definite thing. A tangible object you can touch.

I look between them, wondering how Mom will react. She's got a couple of tattoos herself, so I'm not worried about her judging him based on that. But he's older and this is all weird.

"I wished you told me during our meeting. Surely I would have figured out who you are when I went to visit."

He shrugs, smiling as he looks down at his hands. "Yes, I know. I figured I would meet you sooner or later. But I knew if you or Emma knew, you wouldn't let me invest." His charming smile lights the room. "Better to ask forgiveness."

"You're right." She raises an eyebrow as she stirs her frothy creamer into her coffee.

I bring the mug to my lips and swallow the warm liquid. *How does he even know?*

"Ashley," I say out loud, without thinking. "Ashley told you."

I'm going to kill her or hug her. I don't know yet.

"Ashley?" Mom looks at me inquisitively.

Aiden smiles. "I'm her big brother."

He sounds proud, and I'm glad they're getting

along better.

Mom claps her hands. "Oh! I just love her! This all makes so much more sense now." She calms and clears her throat. "But still, Mr... Aiden, I appreciate the gesture, but we can't accept such a gift knowing what we know now."

I nod in agreement with her words.

Aiden places his large hands on the table, looking more business than friendly. "It's already done, and I can assure you it's not a gift. You've owned this business for over twenty years. It's not charity, it's an investment. I promise you, it's no big deal."

Her inhibitions melt away and she wipes a tear away. "Thank you. I know I can't talk you out of it, but I will repay you for everything."

He shakes his head. "Investment," He reminds with a smile.

I sit in admiration. *He would do something like this for me?*

Aiden's green eyes glide over the full countertops. "You baked?"

He smiles the sweetest smile before moving to devour some cupcakes. I admire his lean frame in our small kitchen. If he were to move two feet his head would hit the fan.

Mom laughs as she watches him. What she says next doesn't surprise me. She's always been this way with my friends.

Just never a boyfriend. I can't believe I just thought that. Is that what he is?

She watches with a worried mother expression as he picks up another.

"Look at you!" She stands up, pulling pans from the cabinets. "You're starving. You're not heading back to the city tonight. Have dinner with us. You can sleep on the couch. I know it's not much, but it would make me happy."

He takes another bite of a blueberry cupcake. "No, it's more than enough. Thank you." He continues as she's about to turn the burner on. "Thank you, really. But I'd love to eat what Emma made. I missed her cooking around the house." Well, that wasn't subtle.

Mom smiles, giving me a sideways glance. Hopefully, she won't ask about that for a while.

Being the amazing woman she is, she leaves to give us some privacy and tend to her garden. But she leaves us with a parting sentence.

"Regina called and said Caleb invited us to dinner tomorrow night when you saw him earlier. I thought that was sweet. Why didn't you tell me? It's been years since we've been there for dinner." She smiles.

I shrug. *Thanks, Mom.*

Aiden raises his brow at me, but I shake my head. It isn't a conversation we need to have right now.

A very happy Rex jumps on Aiden when Mom opens the backdoor and steps outside.

I laugh as he prances around foolishly. "Get down, Rex."

Aiden sets his food down and gets on the floor, hugging the wagging pup.

It makes me melt. I admire how Aiden, with his long and lean body, covered in tattoos, and a powerhouse of a man is sitting on my kitchen floor, telling Rex how good of a boy he is a million times.

Finally, he sits next to me, his happy demeanor morphing into something different. Sadder and darker.

After a few moments of silence, his green eyes glide over me. "Why did you leave?" His deep voice is stern, demanding answers.

I gulp. "I got scared, and I didn't want to be a burden." I admit, cursing myself for thinking I have the strength to stay away from him. All my thoughts have been utterly consumed by everything that he is since I last saw him.

He laughs shortly. "You are never a burden. I already told you, you're mine. You can't separate us. You can't make that decision on your own." He looks out of the kitchen window and back to me. "I won't allow it, Emma," He states with finality.

I want to smooth the worry lines between his black brows. I did this to him. I feel awful; I knew I couldn't stay away from him. I know I'm his.

"I'm sorry." I lean towards him.

He checks the window, making sure Mom is still outside.

Such a gentleman.

Then he grabs my face in his large hands and crashes his mouth to mine.

I lose myself in him as he kisses me passionately. The moment last mere seconds, but I feel better than I have in days. Just from his touch.

He doesn't bother asking if we are okay, if I am okay with us being together, or whatever it is we are. It's as if he already knows what's in my heart. And to be truthful, he doesn't need to ask.

He pulls away, pushing a stray hair behind my ear. "By the way, who is Caleb?"

I hesitate. I could lie, it's not like it matters. No one matters but him, but I can't lie to him…I never will. If my parents' marriage taught me anything, it was that communication is key. That's why they stayed together for so long. I need to remind myself that whenever I doubt him.

I flip my hand carelessly in the air, keeping my tone nonchalant. "An ex from high school."

His jaw twitches and he lifts a brow. "And your mom wants you to go to dinner at your ex's house because?"

I sigh. "She doesn't know we dated. It's a long story, but to make it short, our parents have been friends for years and we dated in high school. He cheated on me on my birthday. That's it." I smile but his perfectly controlled face doesn't waver.

"Why doesn't she know you two dated?" He asks the question I hoped he wouldn't ask.

I shrug. "She would let him stay over really late when I was in high school because she thought we were best friends."

He shakes his head. "Fucking wonderful. Did he do anything to you back then?" His green eyes bearing into mine.

I look at him confused. "No, of course not. Only you, I've never done anything with anyone but you. You know this," I remind him.

His body relaxes before tensing up again. "So, you never did anything with him at all?"

I hesitate and he leans in closer.

"We kissed," I admit.

Aiden's fist clenches.

I grin. "Honestly, it's cute that you're jealous, but you're the first guy I've ever done anything serious with. And you're a lot more...experienced. If I see one more girl whom you've slept with, I'm going to go fucking crazy."

He laughs, his eyes softening. "First off, hearing you say fuck is hilarious. Truth be told, I don't like imagining anyone other than me touching you, let alone kissing you. It makes me want to put a hole through a wall. As for me, no one compares to you." He leans in closer, kissing my cheek. "No one can do what you do to me."

I smile. "Well, don't worry, because I have no interest in anyone else."

He stands up, towering over me as he snakes his large hands through my hair, pulling me closer. "I know you don't, or I'll fucking kill any man who even so much as breathes the same air as you."

He kisses my lips before sitting back down and crossing his arms. "So why did he invite you to dinner?"

How can he do that to me and then just change the subject? I'm literally panting over here, and he looks calm and collected. Damn him.

I shrug. "Don't know. Don't care."

"Good girl." He scoots closer.

My body heats from his proximity, his scent giving me a heady high.

Aiden's features darken as his eyes drink me in. He looks like he's about to attack me, like I'm his prey. He growls lowly before I feel his hand on my neck, gently but protectively squeezing, letting me know how much he owns me.

I know I'm in for it later.

I grin.

I can't wait.

The rest of the night goes smoothly.

While he refused to cuddle with me during the movie out of respect for my mom, he held my hand firmly. As though if he eased up, I would fly away. I made him a sleeping spot on the couch, laughing when he laid down and his feet hung over.

It's midnight and I can't sleep with Aiden downstairs. I know it's only a matter of time before he comes up here, so I'm already expecting him when the door creaks an hour later. I only have on his shirt and a pair of panties.

His hair is a disheveled perfect mess as he makes his way to my bed silently. His gray sweatpants sit dangerously low on his hips while his black shirt is pulled up slightly, exposing his perfectly toned tan stomach. It's in that moment, I realize he brought pajamas. He knew he was either staying here or we were going to grab a hotel, I love his confidence in us.

I admire his body as he pulls his shirt off and throws it on the floor. The shimmer of moonlight creeping in through my window highlights every well-defined muscle.

He gently wraps my hair around his hands and tugs lightly, guiding me upwards. His mouth encases mine, his tongue devouring mine as we kiss. "On your knees."

Even his whisper is demanding, and hot.

He grabs the bottom of my shirt, as I peer up at him heatedly, and yanks it off.

"Knees."

I obey, sliding to the floor. The hard flooring hurts my knees a little, but looking up at him while kneeling by his feet makes me feel vulnerable, and I like it. He tugs down his pants with one hand while holding my head still. His large member is inches from my face, hard and throbbing, and I gulp at the sight of his length so close to my mouth.

"Suck." His voice is firm and full of authority.

I grip his length in my hands, peering up at him with heated cheeks. "I don't know how." *I think I do but what if I do it wrong?* His dick twitches in my hands.

Aiden smiles.

I hold back a sigh. He looks so good from this angle.

"Put your lips around me and suck gently, I'll help

with the rest."

I obey. Taking the tip of him into my mouth, he slowly rocks in and out. I place a gentle hand on his rock-hard stomach, reminding him that he's been shot and needs to be careful, a laugh escapes him as he moves my hand away.

He keeps a steady pace before pushing himself harder and further down my throat. I gag but he ignores it and continues. The feeling of him inside of my mouth is so new, I twirl my tongue as I suck, he gives me commands and I happily follow. Enjoying the way he's teaching me to please him, and the way he taste. The fact that he has such power over me makes me squeeze my legs to ease the ache. This is so hot.

"No one else's cock will ever fill you. Only mine." He growls.

I look up through batted lashes and watch what I'm doing to him. His hair is messy, and his lips are parted. He looks heavenly.

"I'm so lucky to get to ram my dick down your throat. The only fucking cock that will ever be inside any part of you. Mine. Fucking mine." He moans, continuing his very welcomed assault.

I try to push back, wanting to speak. But he holds my head firmly, not allowing it. He shoves in farther and harder each time I try. I'm dripping wet and whimpering with lust after minutes of this cat and mouse game. I'm thankful it's late, and my noisy fan is on full volume to muffle the unfamiliar gagging currently coming from me.

"You'll never leave me again, understand?" His

voice is ragged and earthy.

I attempt to nod but his grip remains firm, pulling my hair up and down, mimicking the motion for me. The ache in my stomach is too much. Desperately needing relief, I move my hand between my legs.

He chuckles darkly. "No." Pulling out, he captures my hands, bringing them behind my back. "Stay."

I leave them as they are, loving how he commands me to do what he wants. Losing control and letting him make the decisions drives me wild.

"You're being punished. You left me." He growls, coming to my eye level. "When I decide you deserve it, I'll get you off myself."

He sinks his fingers into my hair and tugs firmly yet gently.

I let out a moan.

"Now, suck my fucking dick."

Aiden

I love the way she looks with her mouth wrapped around my cock. It's so fucking sexy watching her suck me off yet so fucking cute as she tries to take all of me. The way her delicious pink lips swell from the force of my cock thrusting into her mouth and her sucking me off almost makes me come undone. She's never looked better.

I groan as the pleasure peaks, ramming into her warm mouth once more before pulling out. I watch, satisfied, as she breaths heavily. I move my hands from her hair to the nape of her neck, fingering the chain of necklace I got her.

I pull her up. The way her eyes gloss over and her lips are smeared with a mixture of my pre-cum and her spit makes my dick throb.

"You like your gift? You'll always wear it?" It's more of a demand than question.

She flushes. "Of course." She goes on her tippy toes, pressing her mouth to mine.

I guide her to lay on the floor. The bed creaks too much. She arches her back, inviting me to take her panties off. I slip them down and gently rub her clit. I graze my hand over her voluptuous tits, kneading her perfect nipples in between my fingers. Covering her mouth when she moans too loudly. I was worried her gagging would wake her mom, but it was too fucking hot to worry about at that time.

I admire the way she looks with my hand over her mouth. Only her eyes are visible as my hand practically covers her whole face. I can tell she likes it as her eyes heat. They roll back as I press one finger inside her. So. Fucking. Tight.

I shove her perfect thighs, replacing my finger with my hard, throbbing cock. Still wet from her spit, I slide into her tight warmth easily and relax. Home.

I never want to stop seeing her like this, trapped and pinned underneath me. I have complete control, just how I like it. Me taking her. The way her hair fans out on her floor is almost hauntingly beautiful. My cock pleasures her to the point her eyes roll in the back of her head, telling me just why she will never leave me again.

My frame is massive compared to her. I know she says she's bigger or whatever, but fuck, she's just perfect. I'm tempted to grab her hips, squeezing them as I ram into her tight pussy. As much as I want to hear her sweet sounds, I keep a hand over her mouth while I fuck her.

I pull out after making my girl cum multiple times. Looking into her eyes, I stroke my cock with one hand while lightly wrapping the other around her throat. She smiles when I squeeze lightly. I'm so fucking honored this sweet girl is a freak for me. I release myself onto the hardwood flooring beside her body. It's a hard decision; her face or the floor. But I know she likes punishments.

"Clean it," I whisper demandingly, enjoying how she shivers from the heat of my breath.

She bites her lip before leaning over to grab a towel from the laundry basket. She wipes my cum off her floor like a good girl. I'm thankful the sliver of moonlight allows me to see her blush.

I pick her up and place her on the bed once she's done and lay down next to her. I admire her perfect body. The way her curves sink into the soft bedding, and how her breasts are the perfect size, and so perky. I bite my lip, stopping myself from assaulting them with my teeth. She would look good with my teeth marks ravishing her chest.

Instead, I focus on the lock. "This means I own

you." I twirl the delicate gold lock between my long fingers.

She gives me a curious look before realization fills her perfect face. "It's a lock."

I put my name on it for that very reason. She's owned by me, as I am her.

I smirk. "It shows that you're taken. I have the key, and it will always stay locked." I trail kisses down her jawline and to the tops of her exposed breasts.

"Always."

Seventeen

I can barely speak after last night, my throats sore. It was amazing and I want to do it again soon.

"Need anything before I go honey?"

Mom breaks me out of my trance, and I cough once, quietly telling her no.

"Bye, Aiden! I'm not sure if you'll be here when I get back, but it was nice to see you again." She directs her soft gaze at me. "Emma, don't forget we have dinner plans with the Millers and Aiden if you'll still be here it would be lovely if you joined us."

I look over at Aiden, noting a mask of anger on his face before his demeanor goes back to his usual coolness. "Actually, I think we're going to head back." I gesture back towards the door and Mom gives a mock pout.

Aiden surprises me then. "I would love to go

Miss. Banks. We'll head back to the city after, right, Em?"

I nod, confused as to why he wants to stay.

"I'll see you two tonight!" She wraps me in a tight hug before leaving.

I bolt for coffee, needing something warm for the ache in my throat. Aiden beats me to it, handing me a warm mug. It's not coffee.

He smirks, kissing me gently. "Sore throat?"

I blush furiously.

"Tea with honey. I made it after I heard you get out of bed. Thank God I didn't fuck you on it. That thing creaks!"

I bring the mug to my lips, hiding my red cheeks. I sip the warm tea, sighing as it soothes my throat. I study Aiden with appreciative eyes, even in the early morning, with his bed head and bunched up shirt, he looks like a beautiful disaster.

I pull my lower lip between my teeth as images from last night flash in my mind and a dull ache grows between my legs. A low growl emanates from his chest as he backs me against the counter, capturing me in a kiss filled with such possessiveness that I shudder under his wandering hands. "Careful." I tell him, reminding him of his wounds that he keeps forgetting about.

Aiden sets my coffee cup on the counter before grabbing my thighs and lifting me onto the counter. I yelp as he impatiently spreads my legs apart. I run my hands through his messy hair as he plants wet kisses along my jawline. It is unlike his normal behavior. There's no rhythmic motion to his actions, no hands sliding lustfully along my body. It's as though he lost control.

His eyes are wild as his rough hands grip and squeeze every inch of me possessively. He grabs the back of my neck and angles my head back, providing himself with a clear view of my neck.

I moan as he sucks on the sensitive nape of my neck. I pull away to catch my breath. "You can't give me a hickey now!" I swat playfully at him.

He groans, his wild emerald eyes raking up and down my body. "Why the fuck not?"

When I move to close my legs, he places two firm hands on them, stopping them from moving. "Do not close your legs, Em. Open." He kisses my lips softly. "Open for me, Em. You always keep them open, sweet girl." He grips my thighs. "For me."

I bite my lip, as the ache grows, and desire floods my body.

He glances down at my hardened nipples and growls. "That's it."

Yanking my panties and shorts off, he nudges my legs open and takes me on the counter. He holds me tight, leaving his marks on me. I struggle to pull away, not wanting him to leave marks where Mom can see. Yet he keeps trying.

Growing impatient, Aiden wraps my hair around his hand and tugs my head to the side roughly and firmly. He bites and sucks possessively on the tender skin of my neck, his harsh stubble scratching me in the most pleasant way. His grunts and moans stoke a burning sensation in my stomach.

I want to argue with him, to pull away or push him away. But the way his fingers gently slide over my panties, stroking my clit, turns me into a speechless mess. Besides, my throat hurts too much to protest.

I glance in the mirror after he's satisfied, grazing my fingers along the sore skin. My neck is dotted with markings.

He wraps his arms around my waist and growls into my ear, his voice earthy and husky. "You'll be sorry if you put any makeup on that tonight."

What is that about?

Aiden

If it isn't for the text Emma received after falling asleep in my arms, I wouldn't be going to this fucking dinner party. But he needs to see that she's spoken for.

The number wasn't saved but the second I read it; I knew who it was.

'Can't wait to see you tomorrow night.'

I laugh. He has no idea whose girl he's texting. It's innocent enough but the next text made my blood boil.

'Maybe you can stay over after dinner? I want to see you bite that lip again ;)'

I almost woke her up to interrogate her but she's tired and I trust her. I still remember her whimpers and small screams last night as she slept, probably from a nightmare. I played with her hair as she calmed down.

I wait for Emma to come downstairs so we can

head over to this idiot's house. So help me, God, if she walks down in anything other than a very conservative dress, I'm telling her to change. Thankfully, she doesn't, and she looks adorable.

As much as I want him to see her perfect skin ravished and purple with my marks, it wouldn't be appropriate. I get it but, fuck, I need everyone to quit trying me. Besides, showing my marks means she'll have to wear something with a low neckline and I'm not having that.

"Ready?" Emma asks. I shake my head discreetly. "We'll be a few minutes, Mom."

"I'll meet you two there." Pamela waves and walks out of the door.

I bring my thumb to her lips and wipe her pink lipstick off.

"Hey." She exclaims but doesn't argue, practically bouncing out of her shoes.

"Why are you so hyper?"

"Not hyper, nervous. Why didn't we leave with my mom?"

I grab her hand and twirl her when she inches closer to me, giving her an appreciative once over. My necklace looks beautiful against her soft skin. I adjust it so that it's more prominent. "Just wanted to study you." I tell her, tilting my head down to plant a kiss on her cheek.

Opening the door for her, I head towards the car.

She shakes her head as she points across the street. "They live there."

I laugh at the proximity of their houses. I wonder

how many times he tried something with her, and she declined. Even though they lived so close together, he never got to do anything with her. She declined every guy that's tried her entire life, until me. As though she was waiting for me all along.

We walk in and are immediately greeted by his smiling parents. All the while, my arm is firmly wrapped around her waist, staking my claim. I watch in satisfaction as Caleb's eyes go wide with shock at the sight of me. We greet them back before heading for the dining room. Pamela finishes setting the table before the parents go to grab some wine in the kitchen.

The fucker approaches us then. "Hey, I'm Caleb."

I pull my arm away from Em's side for a moment to shake his hand and pull him close. He's short and I have to lean down to his height.

Quietly, I say, "If you ever text *my* girl anything like that again, I will pound your face into the cement."

It may be overkill, but the horrified look on his face tells me he understands the gravity of my words.

Or not.

I place my hand gently on the soft skin of her neck and whisper, "Throat still sore baby?"

She turns crimson and giggles at me, swatting at me to stop.

I enjoy the awkward silence as the scrawny fuck wiggles around in his seat. Good, I make him uncomfortable. I spend dinner watching him as I talk business with his father. I see him sneak glances at my girl. *Mine.* She's my fucking girl.

Didn't I already threaten him?

I want to reach across the table and beat the fuck out of him. Grab his stupid blonde hair and slam his skull against the wooden table until he can't see. So he can never look at her again.

Once the parents exit to the kitchen, I do the next best thing I can think of.

When I see him glance at her chest – even though her dress is a high neckline, her tits are so nice and perky they're just out there – I slide my hand up her upper thigh. She bites her lip, exactly what I wanted. Emma has barely acknowledged him since we got here and, at this moment, she's looking at me.

But I'm not looking at her just yet. I want to tell Caleb the reason Emma isn't speaking much is because her throat is sore from my cock last night. I fucked her throat so hard that every time she speaks or coughs, she can still feel me deep down her throat. And the reason she is walking funny is because I pounded her tight pussy hard last night while she obediently laid on the floor for me.

But I will never say those things and give him a visual of her. He can imagine all he wants, but he will never get to see her that way. I don't want her to feel awkward, and he's not that important to have a man to man conversation with. Besides, he's hardly a man considering he cheated and hurt my girl.

Caleb watches her lower lip before turning his

attention to me.

I glare him down with an expression that could kill, before turning to my angel. I cup her cheeks protectively with one hand as she puckers her lips out for a kiss. Instead, I pull her bottom lip between my teeth and nibble. I stop before she moans. I won't let him hear such a beautiful fucking sound.

I grab the back of her head and tilt her face up to mine. Gently, I melt my mouth around hers. Before my lips leave hers, I make eye contact with him, watching his face turn blood red. He hastily gets up from the table and I laugh deeply before returning my attention to Emma.

Eighteen

A iden holds the door open as we step inside. I'm glad dinner was early so it will still be somewhat light out on our way back to the city. My mom stayed to help Regina clean up so we're waiting to say goodbye to her.

Aiden grabs my bags from my room and places them in my trunk, before going around the house and looking at the photos of me as a child. He offered to drive me back to Portland and get someone to tow the car, but I refuse to let him spend more money on me.

My stomach clenches as he picks up my favorite picture off the mantel.

He examines the photo of Dad, Mom and I.

We were camping that summer. I was about twelve. My awkward bangs sat above my cheesy grin and my parents looked so proud on either side of me. It was the last vacation we went on before he passed away.

Aiden walks over to me, the picture in his hands. "Love the bangs," He jokes.

I can't help the giggle that escapes my throat.

His voice turns more serious. "I'm sorry about your father. Ashley mentioned his passing when I asked her about you." He gives me a weak smile.

"Thanks, it's okay." I give my usual response.

He carefully sits it down on the mantel before pulling me in a tight hug. "Don't do that with me. It's not okay. Fuck okay." He pulls back to study my face. "You never have to pretend with me. It fucking sucks losing a parent. Trust me, I know."

I feel extremely selfish. Is he talking about his mom? I look up at him, not sure what to say.

"I know you didn't know. Don't feel bad for not knowing." My heart breaks for him, for us. "I don't talk about it and Ashley wouldn't have told you because I don't like anyone knowing my business. Things have changed."

I want to ask a question out of curiosity, I hope it doesn't upset him. I look down at his black boots and take a deep breath.

He lifts my head. "You can ask," He encourages.

I nod. "How?"

"Car accident." He sighs. "After a fight with my piece of shit father. If she wouldn't have kept coming back to him, she wouldn't have even been there. It was raining and she was so upset, I wasn't there." His profile is haunting as he remembers the tragic day he lost his mom.

Who could understand me more than him?

"Thank you," I say genuinely. "I'm sorry you lost your mom." I kiss his cheek as he holds me for a moment.

I suck in a deep breath. "About my dad—"

He cuts me off. "Baby, you don't have to. I just wanted you to know more about me."

I don't take his confiding in me lightly. I give him a weak smile. "I want the same." I count to three. "He was a detective. A good one at that."

I remember how proud I was, attending awards ceremonies and watching as they decorated his uniform with another pin.

"You would think with the career he had and how many bad people he put away, some cosmic force would give him good Karma and let him live a long life." I can feel the tears welling up. "But it didn't work that way and he lost his life at the hands of a drunk. He didn't go down in some glorious poetic fashion, but a routine call when he was out working late. A domestic dispute."

I hold back my tears, proud of myself for getting this far. "The husband shot him when he got there and left him on the street. Just left him there. It was winter, and his body was covered in snow when they found him. He died all alone." Sobs escape me and I clutch onto Aiden's chest.

He holds me close, smoothing my hair out, and tells me it will be alright.

I believe him.

We exchange nothing but a silent crushing hug.

I see Mom stomping across the street with a fury that scares me. Did she notice me ignoring Caleb?

"Emilia Achelois Banks!" She scolds dramatically.

Aiden raises an amused eyebrow and I shake my head.

"Were you leaving without saying goodbye?" She places her hands on her hips.

I stifle a laugh at her serious expression. "Mom." I wrap her in a hug. "Of course not. We were waiting for you."

Mom wraps Aiden in a hug after I let her go. He's taken aback but returns the embrace before we walk down the driveway and towards our cars.

Our heads pop up when we hear a truck starting, as we head for our cars. We watch as Caleb backs out onto the street, his window is down, and his eyes are glued to us as he slowly rolls by. I don't miss the way his eyes widen when he sees Aiden's Mercedes. I see Aiden's amused expression as he kisses me on the cheek before landing a swift slap on my ass.

Caleb scoffs before taking off down the road.

I swat Aiden's chest playfully. "Quit torturing the guy." I giggle as he throws his head back in laughter.

"Oh, my. Eww!" A familiar voice screeches as the elevator doors open.

I blush as Aiden pulls away, letting go of my hands which he pinned to the wall. I shiver as I remember the feel of his lips on my neck, his stubble on my skin and his firm arms holding me down as I playfully struggled to get free.

"I can't move." I had complained, wanting to run my hands through his hair.

He smiled against my neck. "I prefer you that way." His teeth grazed my bottom lip. "I might as well take you here."

I peek around Aiden's shoulder to see a grossed-out Ashley. I take his hand and pull him into the living room. Ashley runs over to me as Aiden rubs a hand down his face in frustration.

She rolls her eyes at him before hugging me. "I came to see MY best friend. I haven't seen her in days since she ran away." She pulls back, giving me a stern look.

"I texted you constantly," I remind her. But from the way her eyes shimmer, I can tell it isn't enough. Mine are burning too, I feel the same way.

"I'm so happy you're okay. I'm sorry I left. Everything happened, and I just kind of just blanked...I'm sorry." I say in a small voice.

She wipes her eyes and shakes her head. "I get it, Em." She rubs my shoulder sympathetically. "We're okay though and look!" She gestures over to a man I hadn't noticed. He's extremely tall with a serious expression stuck on his face.

Ashley grunts. "Moore, please smile at Emma so you don't scare her." She laughs as he gives us a small smile before turning his eyes to the elevator.

"Bodyguard?" I look at Aiden in question, to which he puts his hands up in innocence.

Ashley launches into a tirade and gushes over Ricky. She's been helping him heal from the gunshot wound to his leg, updating me every time I texted her asking if they were both okay.

It's so nice to hear about a guy who keeps her interest and makes her happy. Normally, the men she chooses aren't the best fit for her. I hope Ricky will bring a more stable and happier change to her life.

She heads over to the fridge and grabs a water bottle. "I missed you, Em. Come stay the night with me at Ricky's!" She squeals.

Before I can speak, Aiden's laugh bellows through the room as he makes his way to my side. "Absolutely not."

She swats his arm, pouting. "She's my best friend, Aiden. You can't just decide for her."

I laugh at their sibling rivalry over me.

Aiden brings his hand to the back of my neck. "Give me an hour with her, and then you can take her with you."

Her face contorts in disgust. "Eww. Okay, that's my cue. Bye!" She runs out the door, a serious-looking Moore locking the door behind her.

I scoff. "I'm not having a bodyguard with me, twenty-four seven."

Aiden studies me before smirking. "Emilia Achelois Banks, don't use that tone with me!"

I sigh, throwing a dramatic hand to my forehead. "Please don't ever tell anyone that," I beg.

He pulls me tightly to his body. "Your secret's safe with me. But you know, your middle name has meaning."

I nod. "Yeah, yeah, it means goddess or something."

"Actually, it means she who washes away the pain. You're named after a goddess." He kisses my cheek. "How fitting."

I blush. "My mom is big into astrology and all that. She's a romantic." I smile.

"Seriously though, you will have a bodyguard with you at all times, when you're not in my view." He presses his lips to my forehead.

I nod. Anxiety shoots through me as I realize why I need a bodyguard. That night comes rushing back, but I take a deep breath and push my hand through my hair. It feels greasy and tangled. I shiver at how awful I must look.

"I'm going to go jump in the shower."

"Want me to join?"

As much as I want him to join me, I shake my head, blushing.

Aiden's emerald eyes rake up and down my body as I step into the kitchen, dressed in a short gray robe he bought me. He walks over, dressed in just a pair of basketball shorts, and places his hands on my waist.

"I knew this would look perfect on you." He trails his hand against the fabric, grazing the side of my breast. "How bad did you freak out when you saw it hanging next to mine?" He laughs.

I swat his arm. "That wasn't funny," I scold playfully. "But thank you! I love it. It's so soft!" I caress the material.

He kisses my neck before pulling away. "Where is my necklace?"

"Bathroom." I smile.

He stalks away and comes back seconds later, twirling it around his fingers. "You're not to take this off, baby." He turns me around and places the chain around my neck.

I shiver as his hand grazes my throat. How can something so simple be so sensual when Aiden's the one doing it?

"Better." He turns me around and plays with the lock.

We stare at each other for a long moment.

I wonder what my brain was thinking when I first left. *Was it shock? Or fear of being so desperately dependent of this man?* "Weren't you worried I would refuse to come with you?"

"No."

Oh, the confidence. "Why?"

"I see the way you look at me. You're just as crazy about me as I am with you." He places a solitary finger under my chin, making me look up at him. "Besides, I'm too selfish to allow you to leave again." He plants a kiss on my cheek that sends a shiver down my spine. "Understand?"

His hands trail lower.

I swipe his wandering hands away reluctantly and gesture around the room, trying to calm my breath. *Get it together, Em.* "Are we safe here?"

His inked hands cup my face protectively, warming me. "Don't you worry about that. I know I fucked up, but I promise you, Emma. You will always be safe with me."

I give a small smile. "I need more than that."

He drops his hands. "We buried Maxon while you were gone." He bows his head.

I suddenly feel horrible for being so concerned with myself to think about Maxon or how Aiden must feel about losing his driver, but most importantly his friend.

"I'm sorry." I place my hand on his arm.

He gives me a weak smile. "As far as the Mafia goes, all loose ends will be tied up soon. Nothing to worry about."

"Umm, you still work for a lot of bad men," I remind him.

He shrugs and holds a solitary finger up. "Let's make it clear. I work for no one." Authority laces his voice, making me shiver.

He's right; he deserves the credit of how successful he is on his own.

"And that was my only dealing with someone who would fuck with me. They're all dead." He smiles. "No one else would think of coming after you when word of what happened gets around."

"I'm not worried about me. I was scared, but I'm terrified of you saving me again and getting hurt. That's why I left. You charged in that room without fear for your safety." I try not to cry as he looks at me with the softest expression.

"I know you're worried about me, sweet girl, but please don't." He plants a kiss on my cheek.

"Why did they come after you in the first place?"

He sighs, running a hand over his face. "I was careful since I was dealing with the Mafia. I didn't want to put myself as the sole investor into their 'jewelry business' in case something went south. They buy storefronts and run them as jewelry shops or whatever they choose, but it's a front for money laundering."

"I decided to bring another person in to do the heavy lifting, someone who was familiar with their world. I thought I could trust him, but I was wrong." He props his elbows on the countertop.

"Long story short, Vinny had a daughter. She was only sixteen. My guy, Frank, went to their house one night to get him to sign some papers. They weren't home, but Vinny's daughter was. Some things happened and they got romantically involved. Fast forward a few months, Vinny's daughter, being the young girl she was had already moved on to another guy and wanted nothing

to do with him. Frank didn't like it too much, so he..."
He pauses, studying me. "He killed her."

I gasp.

He sighs. "Last time I'll ever use someone I don't know personally to invest with me."

I shake my head. The poor girl, "But that's not your fault."

"To them, it is, or was. The Mafia works like a family. In their mind, anyone you do business with is family. So, since I did business with Frank–"

"They look at you like you're his family."

He nods. "An eye for an eye."

"Is there anyone else I should be worried about?"

"No, we got rid of the bodies. Nothing can be linked back to us. But, just to be sure, I hired security to follow you and Ashley around at every waking step." His face grows serious. "I'm going to be busier than usual, and we need to move. Between the guy that came here and everything that happened, I want us to live some place new."

I nod, but a frown settles on my face. "Aren't you sad? You literally just got the place."

He shrugs. "I don't give a shit where I live, as long as you're there." He looks at me intently.

It melts my insides. Could I live with him?

We make our way onto the patio, into the warm summer air. Aiden grabs two stemmed wine glasses and a bottle, and pours two glasses of wine.

"Giving alcohol to a minor now, are we?" I tease.

He pulls the glass away. "I mean, if you don't want it."

I stick my hand out, and he returns the thin stemmed glass to my hands. I take a sip; it's slightly bitter but sweet. I definitely prefer it to liquor.

He eyes my happy expression. "You like wine?"

"Very much so. This is delicious! It tastes like dessert!" I take another sip.

He tops off my glass. "Just drink it slow, so you don't get sick." He gives me a sweet look.

"Aww, such a gentleman." I gush.

"I don't want you throwing up on the white rug in our bedroom." He jokes, planting a lingering kiss on my lips.

"Our room," I whisper.

Tall buildings and city lights try to dominate the backdrop, but nothing looks as powerful as Aiden as he sits with a glass of wine in one hand and my hand in the other.

"You can stay as long as you like, you know."

"I'll have to go back to school eventually."

He scoffs. "You're not going back to that school."

I sit up straighter. "What?" *I couldn't have heard him right.*

"You heard me." He gives an arrogant smile.

"But Ashley—"

"No. You're not going to sit here and worry about everyone else. Not your mom or Ashley. You always do that. You put everyone in front of you. I won't allow it." His voice is firm as he flattens his palm on the table. "With the exception of me of course." He winks.

I try to speak, but no words come out.

He places his hand under his chin. "What do you want to do with your life?"

I know where he's going with this.

"Business," I lie. A random major I chose after seeing the prices of culinary schools.

He laughs, knowing I'm not being truthful. "Don't lie to me. I see you. I know what makes you happy."

From the way his green eyes bear into mine, I can tell he can see every inch of me, and all of it is for him. I'm putty in his very capable hands.

He waves his hand in the air dismissively when I stay silent, slouching in his chair. "I already have you scheduled to tour a culinary school."

He's amazing but I can't. "I know my mom's doing good now. Thank you by the way, that's freaking amazing of you. But culinary school is expensive. Trust me, it's the first school I looked for. There's just no way."

"About that…" He tilts his head.

"What did you do?" I scoot my chair back, my voice close to a shriek.

"I wouldn't give a fuck if you didn't go to school or work but…" He smiles.

I laugh. "You're not going to be my sugar daddy."

His eyes darken as he scoops me up and sits me on his lap.

I roll my eyes as his eyes rake over my body. "Aiden, get to the point." I swat his wandering hands.

"You could stay here and bake for me all day." He trails a finger down my leg, igniting a flame inside me. "And then you could wait for me to come home and…"

I swat his arm playfully.

He put his hands up in innocence "I need an assistant."

"Oh? An assistant position would never put me through college. I know what you're trying to do. Maybe I can waitress at one of the upscale restaurants near my school. Ashley works at one and they pay well. I can keep attending business school, and maybe just take some classes at a bakery." I sigh, wistfully dreaming of something bigger for myself.

"She quit." He states.

That is news to me. Why hasn't Ashley told me?

"She's planning on telling you tomorrow. She's thinking of staying here but she wants to get your opinion first. Just don't tell her I told you."

It's hard to concentrate on our conversation when I'm straddling Aiden in a robe with only my panties underneath.

His voice is as velvet as the wine. "Besides, why waitress and deal with a shitty boss and horrible hours just to take a few electives when you can work for me? I'll pay for any school you want."

"True. But still, I won't just let you put me through school. I mean, how can I move here when my whole life is there."

"Your life is not there, Emilia. I'm here." He states. The way he says my full name makes me smile. "Besides, you don't have family near that school. I definitely don't want you around the fucking idiot of an ex-boyfriend anymore."

"I'll think about it." I hold up a finger when he smiles. "But I'm going to look for my own job." He sighs, grabbing my thighs. "Only because I know you'll pay me unfairly and treat me better just because I'm..."

He lifts my chin. "Just because you're what, Emilia?" His voice is husky as he slides my robe off partially and kisses my bare shoulder.

I take my bottom lip between my teeth and shrug, wanting him to say it.

"So many things I can call you." He slides a hand up my thigh.

"My girlfriend?" He trails a long finger up my inner thigh, torturing me with his teasing.

"My fuck toy." He growls, sliding my panties to the side and slips his finger in.

I wrap my arms around his neck, whimpering as I rock my hips while he slowly pumps it in and out of me.

"But I prefer mine." He growls, carrying me inside. He holds me tightly as I keep my legs wrapped around him. We're insatiable, neither of us can keep our hands off each other. "No more questions tonight, understand?"

I moan as he fingers me while he carries me. So strong and effortless.

I melt in his arms as his husky voice rumbles in my ear.

"All I want is to fuck you senseless tonight."

Nineteen

I stretch lazily against the silk sheets. I get up in a daze and pull on my robe. My eyes slide to the clock on the nightstand. Nine twenty-two. Aiden left for work hours ago. I feel guilty I didn't get to see him off. But I'm so thankful we had some one on one-time last night, it's always so perfect when we become tangled in the sheets together.

The elevator chimes as I stumble into the kitchen to get some water. Assuming it's my bodyguard, I walk over to greet him. His back is to me as he stands rigid in the elevator.

"Sir?"

He doesn't respond.

Puzzled, I reach out tentatively, shrieking when his body falls back and thumps against the hard floor. I stare into his lifeless eyes, blood oozing out from a hole in his head. My stomach clenches.

Terror courses through me when a smiling Lucio Matarazzo steps over the prone body and waltz through the doors.

Didn't Aiden kill him? He shot him in the chest. Did he wear a vest?

Oh my God.

No time to think, I spin around and run for the bedroom. My eyes dart around in search of my phone, but I don't see it. Hearing his heavy footsteps coming for me, I rush into the bathroom and lock the door.

I'll hide in here until Aiden gets home.

My hope vanishes when I hear wood creaking. No, not creaking. Breaking, and snapping. My eyes widen as the heavy wooden bathroom door dips in, forced opened with brute force.

Lucio stands in the doorframe, laughing. With quick movements, he makes his way to me.

I tremble in fear, but I can't move. He brings a greasy hand to my throat, lifting me off the cold bathroom. I tremble as he tucks a stray piece of hair behind my ear, a smile taking over his lips.

"Oh, sweet girl." His words are heavily accented; his Italian features dark and sinister.

A shimmer catches my eye and I look down. A sharp blade sits clenched between his hands. Fear courses through my veins. Not for me, but for Aiden.

"Please, just kill me. Don't hurt him," I beg. The words are distant, everything feels distant.

He laughs in my face. "Oh, that's what I plan on.

Killing you and sitting by your dead body until your lover arrives home to find you bled out on the floor." He smiles.

I clench my fist to hit him, but before I can move, he plunges the long knife into my abdomen. The feeling of the metal slicing into my skin makes me shriek in terror and inexplainable pain. I look down as he twists the knife inside my stomach. How have I not passed out from the blood loss and pain? Shock halts me as I stare in disbelief, watching as blood pools and stains my robe. A blood-curdling scream echoes throughout the room, begging for him to take it out.

Why is he twisting it? Why is this happening to me?

"Get it out!" I scream.

He laughs maniacally, before pulling it out and plunging it into my side.

"Get it out!" I cry.

I close my eyes, not wanting Lucio to be the last thing I see before I die. I think about Aiden, his smile that he reserves only for my eyes. How his serious demeanor changes when I walk in the room.

I gasp as I feel the knife being pulled out before it finally plunges into my heart.

Then, everything goes obsidian.

Aiden

My wandering thoughts screech to a halt when the morning's quiet is shattered by Em's blood curdling scream. I flick the lamp on.

Emma is trashing against the sheets, yanking at the material over her stomach. "Get it out!"

What a nightmare she must be having.

I straddle her, pinning her arms to her sides so she doesn't hurt herself, whispering soothing words as I urge her to wake up.

"Get it out!" She screams.

Steeling my voice, I order her to wake up.

She listens, but her eyes remain tightly shut. "Please, Lucio. Please stop." She sobs quietly, her body limp under mine.

"Baby, it's me, Aiden." I croon to her calmly. I wrap her in a hug, pulling her onto my lap.

Her cries slow down and her breathing soon regulates.

"Does that happen a lot?"

She nods.

I throw my head back. I'm even fucking up her sleep. I hate myself. "I'm sorry."

She buries her face into my chest, shaking her head furiously. "Don't apologize. That one was just really bad."

I think back to the other night at her mom's house. She had stirred in my arms, a scream escaping her lips. I pulled her close and managed to calm her down.

Fuck. I should've known.

Smoothing her hair, I keep my voice strong and calm. "Why didn't you tell me?"

She sighs. "I didn't think it mattered."

I roll my eyes. "Emilia, if anything ever bothers you like that, I need to know. What...what happens in your dreams?" She begins to cry again, and I almost tell her she doesn't need to tell me. But I wait patiently. I need to know so I can help her.

"It's...it's different every time. But Lucio, he..." Her breath catches. "He stabbed me."

I pinch the bridge of my nose in an attempt to rid my brain of the visual. "He's dead, baby. Ricky checked every lifeless pulse in that warehouse, just to be sure. No one will harm you," I assure her. But she continues to shake in my arms.

"I want you to see someone for me, baby."

She lets out a small laugh. "What? Like a shrink?" She lifts a brow.

I nod.

"Aiden, you can't be serious." She pulls away, rolling her eyes.

"I wasn't asking, Emilia."

She doesn't put up a fight and instead crawls on top of me.

Being a little late to work won't hurt anyone.

I kiss her collarbone and rub my thumb against her perfect pout, before carrying her to the bathroom to draw her a bath. I'm thankful my bathtub is large enough to fit two. Once the tub is mostly filled, I undress the both of us before depositing Emma into the warm water.

I smile when her rigid body visibly relaxes as the warm water and bubbles envelope her. I wish we can do this every morning.

"You're so fucking perfect." I rub her feet, my eyes glued to how beautiful she looks in the morning. Her messy hair and sleepy eyes.

She smiles, but it doesn't reach her eyes.

"Hey look."

Her eyes dart to my face.

I bring the frothy bubbles to my chin and make a foam beard, eliciting a giggle from her. What the fuck is she doing to me?

She needs peace of mind. She trusts me enough to come back with me.

I have so much shit to do to ensure she's as safe as possible. I'm going to be busier than usual.

This girl, with her smile and slight attitude. Her courage and her beautiful looks as well as her smarts. She is the most important thing in my life. I don't want her to feel anything less than happy at all fucking times.

I don't give a fuck about myself.

But, her?

She is everything.

Aiden surprises me when I step into the kitchen. His suit is tailored perfectly to his lean frame, and the dark as night material looks perfect against his tan skin. I kind of wish I took his offer as his assistant so I could see that all day. But I need to do this on my own.

I found a few affordable colleges in the area. It may be a quick judgment to move my life here, but Aiden is right. I have nothing in Corvallis. Ashley is here. It's not like I loved my school and, as a bonus, there are more opportunities here.

I'm also seeing someone about my nightmares. The medicine is helping and talking to someone is nice but what I really need is for Aiden to be home. His late nights are starting to take a toll on me.

I smile as I head towards him. "I thought you left while I got ready."

He smirks, placing his warm hands on my hips. The fabric of my dress does nothing to mask the perfect heat that radiates from his touch. I'm wearing a form fitting, navy blue dress I borrowed from Ashley a while back. I have an interview for a baker's assistant position today and needed something that screams "hire me". I straighten my hair for a more sleek, professional look. A little makeup and I look alive.

"I wanted to make sure you got there okay. I'm riding with you."

I look over at my guard, standing near the door in his black suit. His salt and pepper hair lays perfectly combed on top of his head while he stares forward. He looks like the British soldiers that stand in front of the castle for hours on end and don't laugh when people jump in front of them. I'm tempted to wave my hand in front of his face, but I refrain.

I lean in close to Aiden, and whisper, "Does he have to come?" I gesture my thumb over to the giant statue.

He smiles, tucking a strand of hair behind my ear. "Even if everything didn't happen, I can't allow you to leave the house looking like this." His eyes leisurely take in my body. "Without some form of protection."

I laugh. "Right." I kiss him. "But can he follow while you drive us? I don't want my new boss to think I'm some spoiled girl who has a driver."

He gives me an amused look. "You're not some spoiled girl who has a driver." A smirk crosses his face. "You're my spoiled girl who has a driver."

I swat his arm. "Seriously. I don't want them to judge me."

He leans against the counter. "Why do you give a fuck what your boss thinks? I should be your boss."

I see the shimmer in his eyes and have to refrain from melting. "Be nice."

He scoffs, stepping towards me. "I shouldn't even allow another man to tell you what to do."

Mint and smoke invade my senses, making me dizzy. I look to the side and take a deep breath. "The application says the owner and chef is Avery. She's a girl." I retort, giving him a confident look.

His body relaxes and he nods. "I'll drive you."

My guard follows close as we walk outside. I roll my eyes "Why don't you have a guard?" I look pointedly between us and my guard.

Aiden shrugs. "Don't need one." He pulls back his black suit jacket slightly to reveal a pistol strapped to his waist.

I swat his arm and hurriedly close his jacket; afraid someone will see. "Aiden!" I shake my head. "You know, you could just do business properly and we wouldn't need all this." I gesture to where his pistol sits.

He kisses my forehead. "I'm trying, baby girl."

I take in the modern detail of Aiden's Mercedes along with the middle seat that I can't slide into and sigh. Aiden looks at me with a raised brow, but I shake my head.

Knowingly, he tilts his head and smiles. "You prefer the Challenger?"

I smile and agree.

He nods his approval, pushing a button on the dash, the sleek car quietly comes to life and we take off down the road.

I point out the directions as my guard follows in a black SUV. I'm beginning to feel guilty for complaining about having a bodyguard, but this is all so weird to me.

"I'm sorry I may be working over here and your detail has to come with me everywhere." I frown.

He slides a warm hand on my thigh, his eyes still on the road. "No, I'm happy. I want you to live your life however you see fit. You won't even notice he's there."

Aiden parks out front and opens the door for me. I climb out with his help and he plants a kiss on my cheek.

"Do you need me to come inside?"

I laugh. "Absolutely not. Get to work. I'll ride back with British soldier guy whenever the interview's over."

"He's American?" Aiden says, giving me an odd expression. I realize what I said. No time to explain, I shrug and kiss him on the lips to say goodbye before turning. He grips my arm firmly and yanks me back into his firm body, he has a serious expression.

He cups my cheek. "No job will ever come before me, understand? Don't rush to say goodbye to me again."

I gulp at the way his eyes burn into me.

He kisses me passionately before pulling away with a smile. "Good luck, baby." He leaves me, breathless, as usual.

I glance at the sign in black cursive.

La Patisserie. A quaint French pastry shop tucked in a small corner of the busy Portland city streets. Modern and beautiful.

Taking a deep breath, I square my shoulders and walk in. I'm instantly hit with a melody of aromas. Fresh espresso and an assortment of pastries and sweets that line the glass counters. I'm getting excited just imagining all the techniques I'll learn from Avery.

Do I call her Miss Avery, or just Avery? Maybe by her last name?

I'm sweating, thinking of all the things that can go wrong and my confidence flies out the window.

A woman eyes me as she walks up to the counter before smiling. Mid-twenties with beautiful blonde hair. She's very accomplished to be so young with her own storefront in the city.

"You must be Ms. Banks," She greets with a wide smile.

"Yes, but please call me Emilia." I shake her hand.

I don't usually use my full name, but I have to admit it sounds fancier. I like it when Aiden calls me by my full name. Hearing others say it will remind me of him.

She gestures to the back. "Right this way, Emilia."

We walk through the small yet spacious shop towards a backroom.

Avery is so friendly I feel like this interview will be a breeze…until she opens the door to reveal an office with a man sitting behind a mahogany desk.

His deep voice bellows through the room. "Ahh, thank you, Miranda." He looks over at me. "This must be Ms. Banks." He smiles.

I try to think of something to say, but he looks so intimidating. "Hello, Mr…" I look at his nameplate. "Moreau."

As soon as Miranda steps away, I walk over and extend my hand.

I'm thankful when he smiles. He looks less intimidating, more youthful. Not that he's older by any means, he just looks so serious. Maybe in his late twenties. Attractive.

His black hair is slicked back, his tan skin creates a sharp contrast with his white outfit. "Please have a seat." He gestures to the leather chair. His French accent isn't too heavy and it's easy to understand him.

We go through the usual mundane interview questions. I sit nervously, trying not to fidget, as he looks over my resume.

"So, you have no experience," He says without looking up from the papers.

I straighten. "While I don't have any hands-on experience in a professional kitchen, this is my passion. I would love the opportunity to show you what I can do." I smile, proud of myself for being so confident.

His eyes rise from the papers and he looks me over with a smile. He stands. "You're hired."

I shoot up from my chair. "Really?" I squeal softly, which makes him laugh.

"Yes, can you start tomorrow? I would say today but…" He looks over my dress. "I wouldn't want you to ruin that dress."

I almost squeal from the happiness I feel, excited about my first real job and to have such an amazing opportunity. He could hire anyone with experience or a degree, but he hired me on the spot just like that.

"Tomorrow is great!" My smile lights up the office.

I can't wait to tell Aiden the great news, but I'm not going to tell him Avery is a man right away. He has to see why this is okay. Nothing will happen.

He has nothing to worry about.

––––––––––––

I fly into the massive building while Howard, my guard, runs behind me. Too excited to knock, I fling Aiden's office door open, a bright smile on my face. I instantly regret it as my stomach drops.

A woman is seated in front of Aiden. She looks so casual and comfortable sitting across from him, it makes me nauseous. Her short gray dress is hiked up where her legs are crossed. Her brown hair swings as her perfect face turns to look at me.

The smile fades from my face as I stand by the doorframe.

"Excu–" Aiden's eyes shoot daggers at the door, ready to scold whoever just walked in without knocking.

His expression softens when he sees me. He excuses himself and ushers me outside, closing the door behind him.

He places a hand on my arm. "Baby? Why do you look so sad? Did they not hire you?" His face contorts with anger.

"I'm so sorry I barged in like that." I shake my head. "It's nothing. I got the job," I say in a small disinterested voice, looking at the floor.

Aiden lifts my chin. "What?"

I don't want to sound childish or stupid. I gesture to the door quietly. "Who is she?"

A smile takes over his face and I swat him.

"You're jealous." He states in an arrogant tone.

I roll my eyes. "No," I lie.

He places a hand on my shoulder. "Baby, I need an assistant."

Why one so pretty? Before he sees my sad features, I smile. "It's fine." I assure him. I trust him. Seeing such a beautiful girl in his office just caught me off guard. It really isn't a big deal.

He raises his brow. "If you don't want me to hire her, I won't." He opens the door and steps inside.

I grab his arm as he edges into the doorway. "No!"

But it's too late.

"Ms. Meyer, thanks for your time." He says simply, shaking her hand. "I have to attend to something important. My front desk associate will call you if you've been hired."

With that, she smiles and walks out.

Aiden ushers me in and closes the door, leaving Howard to stand guard outside.

I sigh. "Is she qualified?" I try not to sound bitter.

He shrugs. "Not really. I don't know. It doesn't really matter."

I look at him with a serious expression. "If she's qualified, you should hire her."

He shakes his head. "I have a lot of applicants to go through. We will see but I don't care about that." He wraps me in a tight hug, lifting me off the ground. "You got the job!"

I can't help but smile. I nod. "I did! It's so cute too. Just what I would imagine a bakery would look like in France." I swoon over the decor and tell him every detail of the rustic exposed brick that lines the shop. "I can't wait to see the kitchen!" I practically jump out of my heels.

"Well, your boss must have really liked you." He smiles. "Avery, is it? Was she nice?" He lifts a brow.

I hesitate. If I tell him, what will he do?

I don't want to lie. I promised myself I won't be dishonest with him ever. I'll tell him after a week…once he sees it's not a big deal, I'll do something sweet for forgiveness.

I want him to trust my judgment and he's been so busy lately that I don't want to worry him.

"She's great! I start tomorrow."

I push the doors open, inhaling the sweet aromas wafting in the air. Howard dropped me off. While I hoped Aiden would have, he was already gone when I got up.

"Ahh, Ms. Banks." Avery smiles, then coughs once. "I mean Emilia. Come." He gestures to the back.

I smile, excited to see the kitchen.

"This is for you." He hands me a white apron, La Patisserie in black scrolled across the front.

I put it on with a smile, reaching around awkwardly to tie it.

Avery takes the strings from my hands. "I've got it."

I've heard horror stories of chefs who yell at their assistants. From the looks of it, I think Avery will be a nice boss. He looked so intimidating at first, maybe I shouldn't judge someone so quickly.

"Thanks!" I wait for instructions, dancing impatiently on the balls of my feet.

He laughs, tying his own apron, "Eager, are we?"

I nod. "This is my dream. I can't wait for you to teach me everything you know." I smile.

He places a hand on the small of my back and guides me over to a working station. I shift from his touch, he's friendly by nature I guess but I hope he gets the hint. "First step. Always wash your hands when you enter the kitchen." He turns the water on. "After you touch anything, you always wash your hands." He checks the temperature.

I do as instructed.

Avery shakes his head. "You need a better lather. Here, let me help." He reaches out, bringing his hands under the water, and rubs the soap up and down my arms.

I instinctively pull away, a little uncomfortable with that type of hands on learning. I don't want to think too much on it, I'm sure he's just a nice man who gets excited about baking.

The day goes by fast, as I learn everything about the kitchen as well as a new technique on kneading dough.

"I know you just started, but as you can tell by the oven, we are in need of upgrades. A company is coming in over the week to install new appliances." He smiles.

I can tell how excited he is. Everything looks beautiful and new in the polished kitchen, but it takes thirty minutes to start and preheat the oven. That won't do when we are busy.

"That's awesome. I bet you'll love having it preheat quickly. So, when will I come back?"

"Friday." He decides after a while.

We continue to work until my hands are sore from kneading dough.

When I slide into the back of the SUV and check my phone, there's one text from Aiden.

I'll be home late. Don't wait up for me.
Again?
Wonderful.

Twenty-One

It's Saturday night and I'm sitting alone on the couch, waiting for Aiden to get home. Howard is at the kitchen table, deep in work on the laptop and quiet as usual. The elevator dings and Ashley burst through the apartment.

I'm happy but my body sighs, I really miss Aiden.

She rolls her eyes as she stands in front of the couch. "Hoping I was someone else?"

I shake my head and feign a bright smile. "Aiden's just been busy. But I miss you too! Come sit so we can catch up." I pat the couch.

A sinister smile takes over her features.

I instantly shake my head, taking her in. Hair done, make up perfect, short dress on. *Oh no.*

"No club," I warn her.

She grabs my wrist, pulling me towards the bedroom to change. "No clubs. Ricky's throwing a party. Come on!"

An idea pops into my head. I want Aiden's attention. I'm too chicken to tell him that. He's busy with work while trying to keep us safe with the new apartment and all. But I miss him.

If Ricky or Howard tells him that I'm at a party, he will come.

Bingo.

"That one." I say as Ashley flings clothes out from the closet.

She nods in agreement before tossing it to me. It's a silver party dress, the back and front are both cut low. If I want to catch Aiden's attention, this is the dress to do just that.

Ashley pokes Howard's chest when we step out of the bedroom, all dolled up. "Listen here, buddy." She snickers as she tries to be serious. "We're going to Ricky's. You call my brother and you'll have to deal with me."

For the first time, I see a smile form on Howard's face.

He looks over to Ashley's bodyguard and nods, "I'll drive the girls."

The party is more packed then I had expected. Music blares throughout the large, upscale apartment and there are people everywhere, all dressed nicely. I'm glad

Ash is somewhere safe and, from the looks of Ricky pouring drinks on the bar top, they party the same way too.

I watch as Ashley's smile brightens when he catches her eye. So cute!

I rest my elbow on the bar top. He still hasn't seen me because he's too busy eyeing Ash. I love it.

He hands her a drink and pours one for himself.

Needing liquid courage, I grab it from his hands, which makes Ashley laugh. His eyes snaps to me before widening.

"Hey Ricky!" I greet with a sly smile.

He stares at me as though I'm an alien in his apartment. He gives me one long drawn out "hey", before turning and pulling out his phone.

Updating Aiden, I'm sure.

Just as I planned.

Aiden

I'm drowning in a mound of paperwork. None of the people I interviewed even came close to earning my trust.

I wish Emilia would have just taken the job. But I get it, she's following her passion. I just wish she'd go to culinary school where she can go somewhere with it. Working in the pastry shop can only do so much. But as long as she's happy, it's whatever.

I've been waiting for her to tell me about Avery. Hasn't she realized I've done an extensive background check on her boss and all his employees?

Fuck. I want to be mad at her, but she's trying to prove that she can handle it herself. I'll lie low until she needs me.

My phone buzzes against the hardwood. My tired eyes watch as it vibrates on the mahogany before I grab it.

A text from Ricky.

I laugh as I read it.

Hey man, Em's at my party.

I don't believe it for a second. She would have called me.

He sends me a picture of Emma standing by the counter, a glass of wine in her hand. But that's not what makes me leave my office immediately. Her dress is cut so low, I can see her delicate back and curves way too easily.

Fuck stopping by the house to change. Guess I'm going to Ricky's party in a suit.

It takes me a few minutes to arrive.

I push my way through the crowd. That's when I see her sitting cross legged on a bar stool. The amount of men surrounding her makes my fist clench. It takes everything in me not to pull up the front of her dress to hide her cleavage. But if I do, her dress will ride up. It's short, too fucking short.

A wide smile takes over her features when she spots me.

I make my way in front of her in a few long

strides. This girl needs to understand that she's mine. Only fucking mine. I will not tolerate this behavior. How does she not get this even now? From the way she brings her bottom lip between her teeth, I can tell she does.

"Come." I demand. Not waiting for her to stand on her own, I grab her arm and pull her up, keeping her body flush to me.

I push through the crowd towards Ricky's room. I open the door to see two naked people on the bed. Thank God it isn't Ashley, or my eyes would be scarred. I shield my girl from the view. I bark at them to get out, watching as they gather their clothes and exit quickly.

I turn to Emma, admiring her full lips and how good she looks tonight. Besides the make-up. She doesn't fucking need it. I wipe the deep scarlet shade off her lips. She's too innocent to be wearing such a promiscuous color on her perfect pout.

"You don't need it," I assure her.

She gives a small smile before heading to the now-empty bed.

"No," I growl.

She looks at me silently, questioning me with her gaze.

"There was another man on that bed. I don't want you on it. Come." I demand. She walks toward me slowly. I notice my lock necklace and smile.

By the wide smirk on her perfect face, I think she has planned this all along.

So, my girl wants to play?

A smirk takes over my face. She didn't wear this

short fucking dress for anybody's eyes but mine. "Do I need to teach you a lesson?"

She nods.

This girl drives me crazy in the most perfect way.

Of course, my perfect girl didn't come to a party to flirt with other guys. She did this to get my attention. I've been so busy dealing with finances, extra security and moving us that I've neglected her. This is her way of getting my full attention.

Well, she's got it.

Emilia looks up at me, the sweetest words escaping her full lips. "I missed you."

That is all I need.

I cup her cheek. The black ink on my wrist is a stark contrast against her perfect and pure skin and the sparkle of freckles that adorn her face. My tongue slides into her mouth, her familiar taste making me harden. I grab the thin material of her dress and rip it down the middle, satisfied when it falls to the floor between us.

"Hey!" She tries to sound serious through her ragged breathing.

"Too short," I state, looking her up and down as I admire her naked breast. No bra but she has panties on. She looks exposed. Exposed, only for me.

She slips off her panties herself, biting her bottom lip as she looks into my eyes.

Fuck.

I lift her into the air, her thick thighs wrapping around my waist. I can't wait any longer. No foreplay.

I want to fuck my girl, to own her.

She gasps as I ram into her tight, wet pussy. It turns me on knowing she's so ready for my cock. My hands grip her ass as I fuck her standing up. The feeling of my arms around her body as she bounces up and down on my dick is intense.

"Aiden." She moans, throwing her head back as I pound into her.

I relish in the feeling of my throbbing cock ramming inside her. This girl is fucking mine. "You like the way I fuck you, baby?"

She moans my name.

"The way I control your body like this?" I growl, gripping her waist as I slide her up and down my shaft.

She is speechless through her desperate moans.

"Tell me who owns you," I demand.

"You…You do." She moans.

I can tell she's getting close.

"Look at you. So obedient. Fuck, baby. That's it. Do you like me pounding into your tight pussy?" I grip her waist, lifting her up and down my throbbing cock. I enjoy how she bounces against my body. I feel her coming undone beneath me. Her body goes slack as my strong arms hold her up.

"Cum for me baby," I whisper into her ear.

Her moans grow louder, and I clamp a large hand over her mouth, so no one will hear her beautiful sounds. "That's right, baby. Cum on my throbbing fucking cock."

And she does, nearly sending me over the edge. Wanting to enjoy her body, I keep going. I can tell she's overstimulated.

"Aiden." She whimpers through ragged breaths.

"Shh, be a good girl. I'm not finished yet."

Her nails rake across my back, her whimpers driving me so close to the edge. I slam her against the wall, keeping a steady, hard rhythm as I pound her tight pussy. I can tell she wants to say something, but she keeps stopping herself.

"Speak," I demand.

"I want you…to…" She moans.

I grip her waist tighter, ramming inside of her as deep as I can go. "What do you want me to do to you, baby?" I whisper in her ear between ragged breaths. She's so wet.

"Choke me," She moans.

Hearing her say the words alone almost makes me cum inside her. Luckily, we're always good about wearing condoms. If my girl wants me to control her and choke her, I'll gladly do it.

My voice cracks as I imagine my hands around her small throat. "If it's too much, just pinch my side, okay?"

She nods.

I continue thrusting, bringing my hand to her soft, delicate throat. My black ink against her milky skin looks sinful. I start off gentle, but she's an impatient girl and leans in hard against my hand.

Fuck. I squeeze harder.

The view I have is perfect. The only thing supporting her body is the wall, my hand on her throat, and my cock as she bounces on it.

"You love when I take you, don't you?" I rub her clit with my free hand, eliciting more whimpers from her.

Deciding she's had enough, I loosen my grip around her throat. She whimpers. I make sure to fuck her rougher and faster for several minutes to make up for the loss of contact.

I pull out and set her on her knees. Taking my cock in my hands, I begin to stroke it after ripping the condom off. "Open."

She obeys. She always obeys. So perfect, so fucking sexy.

I press my dick into her mouth, gripping her hair as she twirls her tongue around the tip. With a groan, I unload myself down her throat. I relish in the feeling of pushing her head down as my warm cum drips inside of her.

She swallows as though it's her favorite drink, all the while looking up at me through batted lashes.

What have I done to this girl?

I help her up and guide her to Ricky's closet. The thought of her wearing anything of his infuriates me. She's only allowed to wear her clothes or mine. Period. Luckily, my girl knows better, and finds some of Ashley's clothes.

She throws on a pair of Soffee shorts and a hoodie before heading to the bathroom. She fixes her hair in the mirror while she wipes away some of me from her soft face.

"I love that my cum is coating your throat right now."

Although she just had my dick down her throat, she blushes crimson.

It's so fucking cute.

Emilia

"I'm sorry I haven't been giving you the attention you deserve." Aiden's deep voice breaks the silence in our room.

I lift from where I lay on his chest and look into his eyes, glad to be home with him. "Don't be. I know you're doing important stuff. I just...miss you."

A sheepish grin appears on his face. "I could tell. Fuck, you looked so good tonight. Next time, give me a warning if you want to play like that. I was about to make your ass so raw; you wouldn't be able to leave the house for a week."

He grabs my throat gently and I ease myself into it. I love that feeling.

He removes his hand and studies me with a smile. "Well, you've got me for a week starting tonight. What do you want to do tomorrow?"

"You took off work?" I jump up and sit crossed legged on the bed. I do a celebration dance when he nods, making him laugh.

"So, what do you want to do?"

I shrug. "Maybe dinner?"

He smiles. "Emilia Banks. Do you want me to take you on a proper date?"

I blush. "Maybe." I laugh when he playfully tickles my legs.

"Well, what are you in the mood for on this date?"

I think for a moment. Italian sounds romantic, sushi sounds delicious but I'm really feeling something more specific. "Hmm, any good seafood restaurants around here?"

He ponders for a moment. "I'll do you one better." He gives me a sly dimpled smile as he grabs his phone from the nightstand.

"Hello. Yes, I'm doing great."

He traces his fingers up and down my bare leg absentmindedly.

"Mhmm." He nods. "I was wondering if you could prepare the jet to leave tomorrow morning. My girlfriend would love some seafood." He winks at me.

A jet?

"Yes, I'm thinking that place we went to last summer with that huge market."

He looks at me with his perfect, dimpled grin after hanging up. "Text Ash and tell her and Ricky to pack for the week."

I gasp. "A week!" I exclaim, surprised. "As long as I'm back by Friday!" I squeal in excitement.

He nods.

"Where are we going?" I hold back my need to jump in his arms.

"Brazil."

He laughs as I pounce on him.

Twenty-Two

The entire experience thus far has taken my breath away.

It's hard to explain the beauty of the private beach house Aiden rented for us. Tucked away in the thick exotic forest against the coast of Brazil, there's enough room for privacy but it's still small enough to be cozy.

It's too dark to see a clear view of the ocean but the moonlight casts a shadow on the obsidian water. I can tell it's going to be a spectacular view when we wake up to the morning sun. The deck outside our bedroom door leads to another bed.

I smile remembering when Aiden took me for the first time on an outdoor bed.

Aiden comes up behind me, moves the hair from

my shoulders, and kisses the sensitive area of my collarbone. "Do you like it?"

I flip around and stare at him in shock. "Do I like it? I love it!" I squeal, jumping into his arms.

The word 'love' coming from my lips makes my heart skip a beat. I hope he doesn't hear my heart beating out of my chest. Thankfully, he doesn't notice.

"Let's head out and sit by the fire with Ricky and Ash!" I suggest.

He sighs, grabbing my ass. "I just want to fuck you all night." He playfully whines as he runs a hand through his hair.

I blush, hesitantly shaking my head. "I don't want Ash to think I'm neglecting her."

He rolls his eyes, placing a firm hand around my neck. "You shouldn't care what anyone else wants from you." He bites my neck. "Only me," He growls playfully.

I tighten my legs at his words. I love how jealous he gets over everything. It's my biggest turn on. I know I'll always win in the end, anyway. I plant my hands on my hips and pucker my lip out, giving him a sad expression.

"Fine!" He throws his hands in the air.

I laugh, leading Aiden outside. I win.

Ashley and Ricky are fumbling with marshmallows while Aiden throws a blanket on the ground. I sit down next to him, admiring his frame as he puts an arm around me. I fit so snugly against him, it's the perfect fit. Ash hands me a stick with a marshmallow on the end and I lean towards the fire.

Aiden pulls me back, "I got it." He kisses me on the cheek before taking my stick and roasting my marshmallow to perfection.

I chew the gooey sugary treat. "You act like I would fall in."

He looks at me with amusement. "You're my clumsy girl." He laughs, planting another kiss on me.

"I'm not that clumsy. Plus, I'm not fragile, you don't always have to protect me." I don't want to tell him I love how protective he is.

He pulls me close and whispers in my ear. "You will never be unprotected. I don't give a fuck if I die. I'll find you and protect you beyond this world."

I bite my lip, looking up at him with admiration. How can he care so much for me? I want to wrap my arms around him, but I refrain out of respect for Ashley. I look over to see her gaping at us. "What?"

She shakes her head and laughs, grabbing Ricky's hand. "I just never imagined Aiden being so gentle with anyone."

Aiden throws a handful of sand in her direction.

She dodges it by throwing a blanket up. "Nice try loser." She sticks her tongue out.

I laugh.

Ricky clears his throat. "So, the bar–"

Aiden cuts him off with a hand and smile. "No work talk. We're here for the girls. You too, Ricky, you deserve a vacation. You're a hard worker and I'm thankful for you." Aiden stiffens as though surprised by his own words.

Ricky beams, grateful to have the support and recognition. "Thanks, man."

Aiden opens a beer for me, and I take a sip. I don't care for the taste but after a few, it grows on me. With a nice buzz, I sit by Ashley on the blanket. I had to pull myself from Aiden's grip, but once I tickled him in front of Ricky and Ash, he practically pushed me to her. So serious in front of other people, but I like it. He's only playful with me.

Her eyes are a little glazed like mine. We laugh as the guys tackle each other on the dark sand. All is perfect. The four of us here, enjoying life. The threat of everything is back at home. Security lurks in the shadows, but I try and forget why they're here.

"I never tell you enough how much you mean to me." I tell Ashley with as much seriousness as my tipsy voice will allow.

"Aww, Em! I love you so much!" She wraps me in a tight drunken hug.

We watch Aiden take Ricky down for the fifth time. Aiden doesn't tire, but Ricky does. We try to warn them of their injuries, but they ignore us.

After a few hours of us talking about life and our plans for the week, Aiden tosses me over his shoulder and carries me caveman style to the room.

I playfully hit him, but he doesn't feel it. "Put me down, caveman!" I yell drunkenly.

Ashley laughs behind us as they stumble in the sand back towards the house.

He pounds his chest with one hand. "You.

Woman. Me. Man." He jokes in a deep voice.

That night, I drift off into sleep with a peaceful trance that I haven't felt in a while.

Happy. Secure. Safe. All in Aiden's arms.

The next days are spent in bliss as we jet ski along the coastline and eat local food from the seafood market. All I wanted was a nice, normal date with Aiden. Look at what he's done for me.

How did I get so lucky?

All the negatives aside, my life has changed for the better since he's come into my life. I was a shell, a naive girl who didn't know herself. I'm still learning, but he's taught me my worth and showed me confidence. He's brought back my drive to follow my passions. Yes, he's protective. Yes, he's possessive of me but that's what I want and need in a man. Especially someone as powerful as him, as sweet as him, as sexy as him.

Aiden and I walk hand in hand down the busy streets of Brazil where the locals have set up booths along the cobblestone streets. I stumble over a smooth, protruding rock at the same moment as a girl bumps into me. Aiden peers at us critically from where the girl and I lay in a heap on the ground, our legs tangled.

She apologizes profusely as I shake my head, laughing at our equal clumsiness.

"It's totally fine!"

Thankful she speaks English because I don't speak a lick of Portuguese.

Aiden relaxes and laughs.

As the couple walks away, I hear her boyfriend laugh as he guides her through the crowded pathway. "Scar, be careful!" He jokes, helping to adjust her dress.

I spot a yellow dress at one of the colorful booths. It looks to be handstitched, made with talented hands. Aiden follows my admiring gaze and asks the woman at the counter for one in my size. I want to argue about spending more money on me.

He looks at the dress and whispers, "That would look fucking amazing on you." His fingers graze my bare shoulders.

Even in the hot Brazilian sun, chills wreck my body.

We head to a zipline park after. My terror grows as we rise above the tall trees of the Amazon Rainforest. I had been confident, but while standing at the edge as a man buckled me into a harness tight, I got nervous.

Aiden stepped up possessively and double-checked his work. When Howard came around and checked it a third time, I rolled my eyes.

"Guys! I'm not going to fly out," I joke.

Aiden crosses his arms in warning before smiling when the man releases the rope.

I scream as I race down and over the treetops, going way too fast. I manage to calm myself after a few minutes to enjoy the view. The lush forest beneath me, and the sounds of animals. The skyline dominated everything. It was unreal.

I grin as Ashley lands on the platform after me. Her normally perfect hair is a tangled mess, which I braided for her while waiting for the guys. Aiden and Ricky are full of adrenaline after the zip line. I don't blame them. It was exhilarating but I'm exhausted and hungry after a long day of fun, Ash too.

It was an amazing thing to see Aiden, who is normally high strung, relax and enjoy himself.

We lay under the stars on the outdoor bed back at the beach house after dinner. A perfect breeze rolls over us. Aiden's sharp features are illuminated by the brazilin moon.

My heart pounds inside my chest. I've never felt this way about anyone. I know I told Ian I loved him, but I had no fucking idea what I was talking about. I didn't understand the gravity of the words then, but now I do.

I've wanted to tell him this entire trip, but I kept chickening out. I know all too well how short life is, what if something happens to one of us? I'll regret every day not telling him how I felt.

How can I live with myself if he doesn't know?

I take a deep breath, hoping to steal some of the confidence he always has.

Aiden

I lift Emma's chin, knowing she has something to say.

She takes a quick anxious breath and whispers, "I love you."

I pretend I didn't hear her over the raging storm. We're protected under the patio as we lay on the outdoor bed. The rain creates a dramatic moment as I run my fingers through her soft hair.

Fuck.

"Aiden, did you hear me?" She asks quietly.

Her heart pounds against my chest.

Please, Emilia. Please don't say it again. I silently plead with my eyes.

She takes a long deep breath. "I love you, Aiden Scott." Her eyes hold her words.

I look away from the intensity of her gaze. She sniffles when I don't respond.

Say something, Aiden. Fucking something. She needs me. She needs me to hold her. But, how can I?

I can feel her holding back her tears beside me. She's so fragile right now I'm scared she will break if I touch her. Thunder roars and the air is thick. It envelopes and traps me, closing me in.

Lightning burst through the sky, illuminating her broken expression.

I need to get the fuck out of here before I suffocate.

I slide out of the bed and throw my clothes on. Her wide eyes follow my quick movements. I pace between the patio and our room, gathering a few things in a haste.

She sits on the bed, her delicate hands wiping the tears from her face. "I'm sorry, Aiden. I di–"

I cut her off with a single hand, not wanting to embarrass her further. "Emilia, please, just drop it okay?"

Her face contorts, a look of betrayal on her delicate features. "I didn't ask you to say it back. But don't ask me to pretend I don't love you." Her voice cracks at the end.

It's like she said it once, and it's all she can say now. Like the flood gates are open.

Fuck, I'm so fucked up. I shouldn't be here.

She deserves more than me. She deserves more than a man who doesn't know what to do when a girl, so innocent and sweet, says I love you to him.

I hastily shake my head, and grab my keys, exiting the beach house from the back, passing her broken face on the way out.

Rain pounds down on me as I climb in the rental car.

I've got to get the fuck out of here.

I hope to find an empty bar. I was wrong.

Too many people fill the space, enjoying their vacations. The open tiki-style bar sits on the sand, with a small elevated deck for the bar stools. A large canopy covers the area, preventing the beating rain from falling on me. The bartender sets down a glass, giving me a knowing look. His accent is thick as he talks while pouring my whiskey.

I breathe in the salty ocean breeze blowing through the bar as I calm myself. I stare into my glass and admire the ice as it melts in the warm air. The rain patters continuously, drawing me into a memory.

I'm standing in the foyer of my grandma's house, dressed in a pair of Spiderman pajamas. The rain falls in sheets outside as I beg Mom not to leave.

"Please." My lip quivers. Only eight years old, I'm afraid of storms.

Mom shakes her head, smoothing out her dress and fixes her lipstick in the mirror.

"Where are you going, Mommy?"

She doesn't answer my question, she ruffles my hair with a smile. "Stay with Grandma, sweetie. I'll be back in the morning. I'll make you pancakes!" She promises.

"Just stay," I beg. I can tell by her outfit and curled hair that she's going to see Dad. But every time she does, he's mean to her and makes her cry.

She leans down and plants a big kiss on my cheek. Her hair smells like honey and her red lipstick leaves a stain on my cheek.

"I love you, Aiden." is the last thing she says to me, before leaving...forever.

I slip the bartender a stack of bills and tell him to keep the drinks coming. I down my glass of whiskey and pull out a cigarette. I fumble for a lighter but a flame in front of my face catches my attention. I lean forward and light my cigarette on the small red-hot flame. My eyes pan to the manicured nails holding the hot pink lighter, trailing further to see a head of red hair, staring at me with glossy eyes.

"Having a bad night?"

I shake my head.

With a cock of her head, she brings her bottom lip between her teeth. "I can help, you know," She offers, grazing her fingers across the top of her breast. "My name's Brandi." She steps between my legs and places her hands on my shirt, her fingers trail across my skin.

I grab her wrist before she goes too far. "Don't touch me." I scowl, but she isn't fazed. Drunk, I guess.

A quick movement behind her catches my eye and I peek over her shoulder to find Emilia staring at us with a blank expression.

Fuck.

Her hair is wet, and her dress is soaked and tight against her skin from the rain. There are too many guys for her to be in here like that.

Did she fucking walk here?

I turn to see Howard sitting beside another rental car underneath an awning smoking a cigarette.

I stand and shove the red head away. She fumbles but catches herself.

Em shakes her head before looking around. Her eyes land on a group of rowdy guys chugging beers.

I laugh, knowing I must be drunk because she walks up to them.

She looks at me once more, hate burning in her honey eyes as a sly smile takes over her features.

I sit back down on the barstool and wait.

243

She walks up to one of them. His drunken eyes graze over her body. I refrain from smashing his head on the table for a few minutes. I clench my fist instead.

"Ouch!" The red head squeals.

I look down at my hand entrapping her wrist.

How did she even get back over here?

"Shut the fuck up." I move her out of my sight, so I can see what the fuck Emilia thinks she's doing.

A round of shots arrives at the table where Emilia is. She downs two, then looks back at me and smiles. It's comical to watch her try to piss me off intentionally. Doesn't she know what'll happen when I get ahold of her?

I snap when a brown-haired guy places his hand on the small of her back. I take a few long strides to Emilia, clamping a hand around her wrist.

One of the drunk guys sizes me up.

I square my shoulders and narrow my eyes at him, satisfied when he shakes his head and turns back to his friends. Smart.

The brown-haired fuck isn't as smart.

He scowls as he looks at my hand on Emma's wrist. "Hey man, I think she's a bit occupied."

He goes to remove my hand.

Remove my fucking hand from her.

I laugh. "I would advise you against that," I warn.

He hesitates before climbing off the barstool and stands in front of me.

I roll my eyes and wait. Just waiting for him to try something.

"Fuck—"

I drop him with a swift punch to the jaw before he can utter one more word to me. How dare he disrespect me in front of my girl. My girl who's in so much fucking trouble right now. With her wrist in my hand, I drag her out to the rental car.

I'm glad we rented an Escalade. There's plenty of room for me to punish the absolute fuck out of this girl.

I open the back door and slide us both into the backseat. I pin her body against the soft cushions, fury raging through me.

"You're going to let another man touch you?" I growl. "In front of me, Emilia?" My eyes are wild as I look for an answer in hers.

The fact that she looks so calm makes me angrier.

"I swear to god I'll walk back in there and fucking kill all of them Em." I spit and she smiles, she fucking smiles at me.

She's driving me fucking mad.

"Get over my fucking knee," I order. Imagining her splayed out over my lap, my hand coming down with force against her bare ass.

She shakes her head.

Cute.

"Now. Fucking now. You want to be a bad girl; I'll punish you like one." I growl.

She puts her finger up, surprising me when she places it against my lips. "No. No, Aiden." She straddles me, her bottom lip between her teeth.

The fuck is she doing?

"You don't have the control right now. I walk in and see some girl in between your legs? Quit talking."

"It's not wha—"

She cuts me off. "I don't give a fuck what you're about to say." She chuckles.

I throw my head back. *What is she doing?* "Don't take that tone with me, Emilia." I grip her waist in a warning.

A soft moan escapes her lips.

Fuck.

"Don't." Her voice is louder than usual.

I want to flip up her short dress and take my hand to her bare ass until it's raw. But the way she looks at me, the way she slowly grinds against my lap shuts me up.

Slowly, she lifts her dress, exposing her thighs. Her body and dress are wet from the rain, but I can see her glistening between her legs. No panties.

"I walk in a bar, after telling you I love you…"

Her voice breaks and she stops. I grip her hips to move her myself, but she swats my hands.

"And then I find some fucking girl in between your legs when I walk in."

Not knowing what to say, I shake my head.

She grabs my face, making me look at her. "What would you have done if that were me? If you told me something so personal and I just left, and when you came to find me, I was standing between some guy's legs? A guy that looks totally different from you," She spits.

The thought of her touching another man makes my body shake. "It's not like you think."

"Well, tell me, Aiden. What's it like then? Because, not only did you have a girl fucking flirting with you. She was a redhead, skinny, and wearing something I would never wear. Is that what you want? Someone who's the complete opposite of me?" Her voice slurs slightly from the shots she previously downed.

I can tell she's trying to be brave but she's breaking. I place my hand on her cheek. "No, baby. There's no one more perfect than you. I pushed her away. I swear I would never." I go to speak again but she covers my mouth, causing me to chuckle.

"If I ever," She looks at me with fury, "ever see another girl in between your legs. I'll never speak to you again."

"Now," She whispers in my ear while grinding against me. "I'm in control tonight. Got it?"

"Yes, ma'am." I smile, giving in to whatever she wants to keep her from being upset with me.

I'm already hard as she unzips my pants. She slips herself over my shaft and my head rolls back from the pleasure. We're both uncoordinated and a bit drunk, but the feeling of her riding me is so exquisite I forget everything else. I fight the urge to flip her around and pound her tight pussy. But what she's doing feels so good.

During her climax, she moans, "You're mine Aiden."

Gripping her hips, I wrap my hand around her throat, reminding her who's boss. "As you're mine."

Twenty-Three

It's our last day here. I still remember every detail of last night.

Deciding I need him to talk to me, I slap Aiden on the chest.

He wakes up with a jolt. "What the fuck!"

His eyes dart around the room before landing on me, my arms crossed and a scowl on my face.

His dimples appear as he looks at me with sleepy eyes. "Good morning, Angel." His velvet voice is thick with sleep.

With the frenzy of emotions from last night behind me and the drunken courage gone, only anger is left. "Why was she in between your legs?"

He places his arm on my leg, and I scoot back. He sits up; his shirtless body, messy hair and ink make me dizzy. I need to concentrate.

He pinches the bridge of his nose before taking my hands. "I thought we talked about this last night."

I roll my eyes. "Yes, but I was drunk." I don't remember much, besides being in control when we had sex.

"Emilia." His tone is pleading as he runs an inked hand down his face. "I shoved her away, I swear. You walked in and she just happened to walk between my legs. I promise you."

His sad tone and glossy eyes make me reconsider my next words.

"You promise? I can't handle if you cheated on me."

He smiles, his eyes blazing into mine. "I would *never* cheat on you."

I calm down. "So, what happened?"

He bows his head.

"Coffee first?"

He throws on a lone pair of gray sweatpants that sit dangerously low on his defined hips before leading me out onto the porch where he drags me onto his lap. He breathes in the morning salt air.

"Em, I can't express how much you mean to me. Hearing those words brought me back to a dark time." He lowers his head against my arm.

I lift his chin up, looking into his eyes to give him strength.

"The night, that was the last thing my mom said to me. Then she was just...gone." His eyes gloss over.

I wrap my arms around his neck.

No more needs to be said, but he continues. "I have never given a fuck about anyone, except you. I'm sorry. I'm so fucking sorry I walked out on you like that. That was a move my dad would have—"

I cut him off with a solitary finger to his lips. He looks so broken, so vulnerable. A stark contrast to his usual serious demeanor.

"Don't apologize, and don't ever compare yourself to him. I get it. Don't worry. When you're ready, you'll tell me. If not…" I think of something to take that pained look away. "If not, it's fine." I give him a reassuring smile that doesn't quite reach my eyes.

His expression is serious. "I don't know if I'm capable of giving you what you deserve."

I cup his face. "You deserve every ounce of me," I assure him.

He smiles a cheesy grin before burying his face in my neck. He lifts his pleading eyes to mine. "Those words have been tainted for me. They'll never be the same. I don't want you to think I don't care deeply about you. I do. So fucking much you couldn't even fathom."

His eyelashes are thick as he looks up at me. "You say those words…" He closes his eyes. "And I…You can't fucking go anywhere, Em. You can't leave me. Ever. I'm weak for you. I'm crazy about you." His emerald eyes shimmer in the rising golden sun. "You're mine, Emilia."

I smile. He's been telling me he loves me in the only way he knows how. "As you're mine, Aiden. Always."

That is enough. Of course, it is.

My phone rings, interrupting the moment. Aiden grabs it, checking the screen. It's my mom. I go to ignore it, but he answers before I can stop him.

"Hey Pamela. Yes, she's right here." He hands me the phone.

I roll my eyes. I told her I was going on a vacation with Ash. She wouldn't care. I'm an adult, but I don't want to have that conversation.

"Hey, Mom." I sigh, waiting for the third degree. My body tenses when I hear her sniffle. "What's wrong?"

Aiden sits a little straighter.

"He's getting released on good behavior." Her voice is hoarse. I can tell she's been crying for a while. I want to ask her who. But from her hysterics, I already know.

The man who killed my father.

Thomas Peters.

Tears slide down my cheeks and I lower my head, asking through gritted teeth, "When?"

"A month."

I hang up after talking with her for a few more minutes, stunned. I turn towards Aiden to explain but he waves his hand in dismissal.

"I heard it. The speaker was loud." He strokes my hair. "I'm sorry."

"When we get back, I want to visit him." I state with a confident nod.

He goes rigid. "Abso-fucking-lutely not. You're not going to prison to visit a murderer." His tone is laced with finality.

I shake my head. "He killed my father. He hasn't even been in jail for five years. Mom said it was good behavior. Fuck that. I didn't have the courage to do a victim impact statement at the trial, and I regretted it ever since. I couldn't even bear to sit through the trial." Tears lace my vision.

"I need this. I need him to see I'm okay, even though he took something so precious away from me. Before he's back on the streets, I need to tell him while he's still locked up in there like an animal."

Aiden nods in agreement, stroking my hair. "Okay, baby. Whatever you need."

I smile as I take in my new surroundings, a sense of calm coming over me. Our new penthouse is furnished with everything from the old apartment, providing an essence of familiarity in the large space. I admire the view beyond the floor to ceiling windows. I couldn't imagine he would find a penthouse with a better view, but I was wrong.

The kitchen takes my breath away. Elegant marble countertops and a double oven. His old kitchen is nothing like this. The equipment is something one would see in a New York steakhouse with the best bakery in the world attached. A pitch-black eight burner stove sits atop the white marble, contrasting perfectly. Brand new mixers and all kinds of baking equipment line the countertops, adorned with dainty red bows.

Our room is modern, and the simplistic decor

makes the space look refreshing and clean.

Tears flow down my face in sheets.

Aiden wraps his arms around my neck and kisses it. "I wanted to make it perfect for you."

With a wide smile, I turn and throw my arms around his neck. Melting in his gesture, in his embrace, in everything he is.

"I'll send you and Howard shopping for some art pieces, or whatever you like." He blushes slightly, gesturing to the few canvases that are on the walls. I admire the paintings, brushing my fingers over the rough surfaces of each one.

I remind myself he's never done this before, neither have I. But for him, he isn't used to showing a softer side of himself to anyone but me. "Everything is perfect, and this art is amazing! Where did you get it?"

A dimpled smile blooms on his face. "Came with the place." He shrugs, "and I want your touch on it."

I smile. I guess this is it. We're officially moving in together. It's not like I haven't been living with him, but this seems more stable, like this is for us. I haven't given much thought to looking for apartments with Ash. We mentioned it in passing, but she's content staying with Ricky. More than content, she's elated.

Aiden leads me up a set of familiar steps. A heavy metal door opens to reveal an even more breathtaking view. We are so high up the stars look closer than ever.

"Look there." Aiden gestures to a corner.

That's when I see a bed situated in a perfect position to look at the night sky.

Tangled and full of passion, that is where we sleep on our first night in our new home.

Well, not much sleep.

I loved every ounce of Brazil, but the looming threat of Thomas getting released has me on edge. He won't come for me; it's not that kind of fear. He's nothing more than a drunk, who has no life in or out of prison. But he deserves to stay in prison.

How can they let him out on good behavior after murdering a decorated officer?

The thought haunts me as I get ready for work. I already have an appointment with the corrections facility for next week. I need to ignore that until it's right in front of me.

Back at work, I try to focus on the task at hand and the positives, clearing my head of the troubles stirring inside. We're safe; our new home is more than I could ever ask for, I just got back from a brilliant vacation and now I get to go work in a kitchen that is stocked to the brim with all new appliances.

I arrive at work to see Avery turning on the ovens. "Wow."

Avery walks towards me, wiping his hands on a towel. "Wow is right." He looks me over and smirks. "You got tan."

"My boyfriend took me to Brazil." I smile brightly.

"Boyfriend?" He half laughs as he walks over to

me, his face serious.

"Yes?" I gesture around the room. "I really love the new equipment!" *Why would he laugh about me having a boyfriend?*

His smile returns. "It's wonderful! They work perfectly. I've been prepping the space to teach you how to make my favorite. Éclairs."

I squeal. These lessons will give me a skill I'll utilize throughout my life.

Avery guides me to a table where a plate of freshly made éclairs sits. "First, we will taste some I made this morning so you can get the flavor profile."

I take a large bite of one with a moan while Avery watches me with satisfaction. "So good!" The made from scratch ingredients change the game.

"Come, here's your station." He gestures to a steel top filled with ingredients. "Get started on the dough, while I start on the chocolate. I know you already know how to melt it down." He smiles as he makes his way to the burners.

I wash my hands vigorously and get to work. I gasp when his body presses against my back as I roll the dough. I go to move but he pushes in.

"In France, we let the wrist do all the work and the hands are just helpers," He whispers quietly into my hair. He brings his hands into mine as he kneads the dough with me. It begins to form better.

"Oh, so I just need a little more elbow grease," I mumble in an uncomfortable tone as I try to wiggle out. I like that he's a hands-on teacher, so I can learn better. But he doesn't need to have his body against mine.

"You're so good at this." He murmurs in a low voice as he leans further in. "A natural." His voice is breathy.

To my disgust, something hard press into my back. I gasp and turn quickly. His hands are on the counter when I face him. He's holding me in. Trapping me. I look around Avery's shoulder, desperate to find an escape. "Excuse me."

A sly grin adorns his face. He tilts his head, studying me. "Don't move. There's so much more my hands can teach you." He smirks.

My stomach drops and I shake my head. "I think I've had enough for today. This is wildly inappropriate. I have a boyfriend." I remind him with a stern, and mildly shaky voice.

He chuckles. "Your little boyfriend isn't here though, is he? I'm sure I can show you a better time." I almost laugh at his audacity but I'm too scared.

His accent grows heavier as his voice raises to a poisoned tone. "Oh, come on. You've been flirting with me ever since you came. Why do you think I hired you with no experience? You were practically begging for it with that dress you wore during your interview." He leans further in.

The cold metal counter against my back makes me shiver. I look around the room, hoping to see one of the girls. But to my dismay, I remember no one was around when I came in.

I smile shakily at Avery. When I feel him relax, I swiftly knee him in the balls, satisfied when he doubles over and falls to the ground. I rush outside and look around for Howard. I smile when I see him hurrying my way.

Standing in at an intimidating height, I let out a breath I didn't know I've been holding when he gets to me. "Howard." I cry, throwing my arms around him.

He stands stiff, not returning the gesture until I sob into his chest. His movements are awkward as he wraps one arm around me. He stares at me in confusion when I step back.

"Can we go home?" I ask, I'm breaking. Too much is happening to me.

He looks me over worriedly. The act is fatherly, not so much of a bodyguard. "Why?" He sounds skeptical, his thick eyebrows bunching up.

I think for a moment. "I got sick and it made me upset?" I lie.

He laughs before gesturing to the phone in my shaking hands. "Call him."

"No." I want to laugh, thinking of how bad an idea that is. But my body is still shaking from what just happened.

Howard shrugs. "Then, I will."

I sigh before hesitantly dialing his number from my phone. I look over at Howard and narrow my eyes. "I'll get you for this."

He laughs, before surprising me when he places a reassuring hand on my shoulder as I wait for Aiden to answer the call.

"Hey gorgeous."

Relief overwhelms me when I hear his voice. Unable to contain my heavy emotions, I sob into the phone.

"Hey, woah. Babe? What's happening? Are you okay?"

I take a deep breath and collect myself. "Yes. I'm fine," I mumble quietly. "Howard made me call you."

"Why?" His tone clipped. "What happened?"

"Nothing happened."

Howard speaks up, "Speaker."

I try to cover the phone but it's too late.

Aiden's voice booms through the phone. "Emilia, what the fuck is going on? Why did he say, speaker? Put the damn phone on speaker!"

I press the button, flipping Howard off with my free hand.

"I'm here, boss." Howard looks at the phone, ignoring my rude gesture.

"What happened?"

I want so badly to hang up the phone, not wanting to bother him with this mess.

"She flew out of the front door in tears, I figured you'd want to stop by and see what happened. She wanted me to take her home and not tell you."

I throw my head back like a defiant teenager.

"What the fuck? I'm already on the way. I'll be there soon." He growls into the phone.

———————

Aiden takes one look at me and makes his way to the bakery.

I chase after him, pulling his arm.

He reluctantly stops outside the door, cupping my face in his hands, and breathes deeply. "You can say whatever you want, but I already know someone in there hurt you. Who was it? Your boss? Or was it a co-worker or customer?"

I sigh, hesitating before looking away.

He holds my face firmly. "Either you tell me what the fuck just happened, or everyone in this building is getting fucked up." His face red, and his breathing heavy.

"You're going to be mad," I state quietly.

"Why?" He tries to stay calm but is failing.

"Avery is a man."

He shakes his head. "I already fucking know that, Emilia. Now, tell me what happened." He growls.

I bow my head in embarrassment.

"Now!" He yells.

I flinch. He's never raised his voice at me before. "He…well…" I stutter.

He strokes my hair, cooing, "Baby, please."

I take a deep breath. "I didn't want to tell you about Avery being a man because you didn't need to worry." I wipe away fallen tears. "I wanted to show you it wasn't a big deal. But things changed when I went in this

259

morning. I was rolling dough when he came up behind me and helped."

I see his body go rigid.

"He leaned against me. At first, it was odd, but then…" I trail off.

He squeezes my shoulder. "Then what, Emilia?"

I lean in and whisper, "He pressed into me and I could *feel* him. Like he was–"

Aiden cuts me off with a finger to my lips. He looks furious as he steps back. His face contorts before he laughs manically.

I don't have the strength to stop him as he throws the door open and steps in.

"Where?" He demands.

I gesture to the kitchen.

"Stay," He states.

I don't listen.

He stops, pinching the bridge of his nose to hide his annoyance, before placing his hands firmly on my shoulder. "Emilia, I need you to stay," He hisses through gritted teeth.

I shake my head.

"No. Absolutely not. You fucking lied to me. You lied about your boss being a man. And now, look what happened? You fucking stay."

I don't argue when he pulls out a chair and gently pushes me down like a child, but I cross my arms. I look at him with pleading eyes, not wanting any more bloodshed. "Don't kill him."

Aiden simply looks at me with a maniacal smile before opening the kitchen door.

I bury my face in my hands.

Twenty-Four

Aiden

I see who I presume is Avery standing over a counter. "Emilia darling, you came to your senses." He turns around, confusion on his face when he sees me.

I study him. The audacity, no, the balls this man has to hire a young girl, and then hit on her thinking she'll never tell is fucking sickening. I own my own business and I'd never use my position of power to get into a girl's pants. It's something that comes naturally to me, which tells me this guy is a sick fuck.

I notice he's holding an ice pack between his crotch. My Emilia must have kicked him in his balls. I would laugh if I wasn't seething with rage.

I put my hand on my chin in thought. "You know what I love." I run my hands along the shelving, knocking the glass containers to the hard flooring. The shattering makes my pulse quicken.

"When a grown man hires a young lady thinking he can have his way with her just because she works for him…" His body goes stiff as my legs glide in front of him. "But that's where you fucked up." I growl, grabbing his throat. "You tried to take advantage of someone very important to me." His pulse on my palm is unsteady and quick.

"I didn't—"

I cut him off. "No, no. You're not about to tell me my Emilia lies. Are you?" He shakes his head and I get in his face. "You have the fucking balls to lie to me? To my face?" My skin is red hot as I bellow.

In one quick movement, my knuckles connect with his jaw with all my power. He falls on the hard flooring and I get on top of him, pummeling him with my fist. I wait for him to fight back as I breath heavily, but he lays there like a bitch.

"You want to try to fuck with *my* girl, and yet when you face the consequences, you cower under me?" A deep laugh escapes me.

He shakes his head.

"You hit on my fucking girl. You're her boss! You sick fuck. Couldn't you tell she didn't want you?" I spit.

He shakes his head and says in a weak voice, "She's lying."

I laugh at his audacity. Perhaps he has a death wish.

Emma may not have told me the truth but that's because she didn't think something like this would ever happen. It never should have. I do the things I do for her own protection. The thought brings fury throughout my core as I pummel my fist to his face until he's unconscious. The blood splatters onto the white flooring.

This is exactly why I didn't want Em to follow. She doesn't need to see this. She still has nightmares from what happened before. Why do these things happen to her? Why can't I protect her from everything? If only I could place her in a bubble and keep her away from the world.

I should fucking kill him, put a bullet between his eyes. Better yet, snapping his neck with my hands would be a satisfying sound. But Emilia asked me not to kill him.

Fuck. I'll get Howard to do it.

Em's eyes widen when she catches sight of my bloody knuckles when I return. I rush to her and scoop her in my arms. I couldn't think clearly through my rage. But now that the problem is half solved, I can breathe.

How scary that must have been for her.

"I'm so sorry that happened to you, baby." I lift her into my arms and carry her outside.

"Do I need to get the body?" Howard asks.

I shake my head. "He's alive. You know what to do."

Emilia whimpers in my arms. "Don't kill him."

Why is she protecting him?

"Why the fuck not?" I put her down.

She wipes her eyes with shaking hands, her tone defeated. "No more bodies."

I sigh before looking back at Howard. "Call Detective Stark and tell him what happened. Maybe Emilia's not the only girl who's been harassed by this creep." I look over at Em and she nods.

I help her into my car, making sure to fasten her seatbelt.

I admire the way the fabric looks against her skin. I like her tied down. Chill, Aiden. She's upset.

I place a hand on her knee. "Are you okay?"

She looks over at me with a small smile. I'm trying to keep calm. A thin thread holds me back from turning this car around and fucking ending that scumbag.

That thin thread is Emilia's sad face.

"Yeah, I am. Thank you, Aiden."

"You hit him in the balls?"

Her smile grows wide, her laughter filling the car. "I did."

"Good girl. One of these days, I'll teach you how to fight." I clutch her hand. "For now, we're going home."

Her smile doesn't reach her glistening eyes. "I'm sorry."

I pull into the parking garage and slam on the brakes. I cup her cheek as I look into her sad eyes. "Don't you dare apologize to me. I'm so sorry that happened to you. It's not your fault."

Emilia

I took a shower once I got home and passed out on the bed. It was dark out when Aiden came back in the bedroom.

I wake to the feeling of him snuggling against my back, but his arm doesn't go around me. I back into him, desperate for his hands to be on me.

He lets out a deep breath. "May I touch you?" He asks, confusing me.

"Why would you ask?"

"With everything that happened today, I'm sure you felt…violated." His tone is dark, and I feel him clenching the sheets.

A small laugh escapes my lips. "Hardly. I was more upset with myself for not talking to you from the beginning. When I think about it, he was kind of off. But I was just so excited to have the opportunity. I'm just so stupid." I run my hands through my hair.

He turns me to him, his face inches away.

If I could lean forward…

"Don't call yourself stupid. You should be able to work wherever you please without some fucking idiot trying to get into your pants." He says with an exasperated breath.

I lift a brow. "What if I work for you?" I challenge him as I look into his eyes with humor.

He smiles. "If you work for me" His hand trails my body. "I can't promise I won't hit on you."

"Show me what you would do to me," I whisper, wanting him so badly that my confidence is through the roof.

All I want is to lose myself in him.

Aiden

I kiss her, holding her body tight against mine.

I think about how much she's been through. The thought of another man's body pressed up against hers drives me fucking insane. I need to claim her body, pound into her and relish in the fact that she is mine. Body and soul, this girl is fucking mine.

But I need to put my anger aside.

Looking at her and the moonlight cascading across her soft skin making her look like a painting gives me another idea. To fuck her long and slow, to make love to her.

I trail my hand up her stomach, slowly and softly all around her body. I pull back the fabric of her robe, giving me perfect access to her soft skin. Grazing her leg all the way up to her neck, I slide my hand across her throat. I resist the urge to squeeze and continue to touch her gently. Her nipples are hard, as I take one between my teeth and graze it lightly. I kiss every inch of her until I reach her belly button.

Her cheeks are flushed, and she pants as she bucks her hips.

I slide her panties off quickly and bury my face between her legs. Taking my time, I pleasure her, enjoying her sounds as I make her body twitch. The way she tugs lightly on my hair encourages me as I swirl my tongue around her opening.

She moans and bucks her hips.

It takes every ounce of strength to not wrap my hand around her throat and fuck her senseless. But I need to stay on track. She needs to see how much she's treasured.

I rise on top of her, bringing my throbbing cock to her opening. Gently and slowly, I slide into her. I kiss her parted lips as she moans my name. Slow movements, grinding and fucking her this way gives me such a good view of the faces she makes. The small whimpers escaping her lips when I push myself all the way inside her fucks me up.

She is just fucking perfect.

Needing to stake my claim, I pull out and stroke my cock above her stomach, admiring how my cum coats her soft skin. All the while, Em looks into my eyes, her lip between her teeth.

Emilia

Aiden looks so peaceful when he's asleep. His thick eyelashes cast a shadow against his tan cheeks. His hard edges softened and his hair a beautiful disaster.

Not wanting to wake him, I discreetly slip out of bed.

He groans and pulls me back. "Where do you think you're going?" His voice thick with sleep.

"Bathroom." I try to wiggle out of his grip, but he simply holds on tighter, planting kisses along my shoulders. "Aiden! I have to pee!" I playfully yell at him.

"Wait." I turn to him. "Last night, when you said something about working for me, were you just playing?"

I smile. "If you'll have me." His face lights up. "I would rather work with you and save up to go to culinary school than have to deal with anything like that ever again."

He rolls his eyes. "You know I'll pay for your school, right?"

I nod. "Yes, but I would rather earn it. You know?"

And just like that, I'm speaking his language. He nods in agreement, before pulling me into a kiss and releasing me. My eyes go wide when I catch sight of the clock.

"You're late for work!" I dart around the room, grabbing his things. I stop when I see his amused expression. "What?"

He shrugs. "You had a rough day yesterday. I took the day off."

"You were just off for a week though. Is that cool?"

He laughs, his dimples deep. "Of course it is. I'm the boss. I can work from anywhere. Now, get back into bed, woman." He growls playfully.

I run away, giggling and he chases me down, hauling me back into bed.

That is where we spend the morning, afternoon, and well into the night.

We ordered room service for lunch, which Howard delivered. I hid under the covers, trying not to giggle as Howard walked in, carrying a tray of food, and exiting quickly afterwards. We ate in bed, carefree, before making love as if it was giving us our last breath while the sun rose and fell outside.

I decided to bake Aiden's favorite, chocolate cupcakes with buttercream frosting, for dinner. His warm arms wrap around my waist as I mix the batter. Howard keeps guard in the living room. Aiden pulls my robe to the side and kisses my bare shoulder.

I watch him walking away, his sweatpants low on his hips. His tan and inked back is a spectacular view. He leans down and speaks lowly to Howard, who then swiftly leaves, as Aiden makes his way back to me.

I continue the task at hand. Pouring the thick mixture into the liners, I place the cupcakes in the preheated oven. I turn to find Aiden with a handful of thick batter. I gasp when he lunges at me, pulling off my robe and placing a swift slap on my bare ass, covering me in the batter.

"No, you didn't!" I scoff playfully. I turn to the batch of icing I'd already whipped and smother his perfectly sculpted chest in it.

"Now, you've done it." He growls, grabbing a bag of flour.

"You started it." I giggle hysterically as flour drifts through the air, like a snowstorm in August.

His carefree laugh bellowing through the room makes my heart melt.

We end up on the floor, covered in batter and icing and flour. We make love as the cupcakes burn in the oven.

An absolute perfect day.

Twenty-Five

It's my third day working with Aiden. From the way he looks at me whenever he passes my door, I can tell it won't be long before he drags me into his office for a little fun.

I'm a few offices down from him. I had thought I would be in the open area near the reception desk, but he showed me this office on my first day. The view is beautiful, dominated by the city's skyline. The entire room has a feminine yet modern feel. White and clean, with burst of color.

I have on a navy-blue dress, short but still business casual. I'm somehow managing not to break my neck in a pair of tall black heels. I went shopping yesterday and got a few new outfits. I attempted to slip away and pay on my own but when Howard saw me, he took my wallet with a laugh and gave Aiden's black card to the cashier.

There aren't too many people in the office. Everyone mostly keeps to themselves, getting their work done. I'm not alone though, my shadow follows me everywhere. I really enjoy having Howard around, he may be quiet but he's respectful. He cares about me. Whenever I step out, I see his salt and pepper hair peeking around the corner, checking in.

My phone rings around lunch time.

"Emilia speaking, how may I help you?" I laugh.

"My office. Now." Aiden says, his tone firm.

I smooth my dress out and run my fingers through my hair before I walk to his office. He looks so sexy sitting behind his large desk. So...powerful.

"Am I in trouble?" I tilt my head with a blush and let out a small laugh.

A half smile creeps up his face. "Door."

I close it behind me, turning the lock when he raises an eyebrow. He beckons me over, gesturing to his lap. I obey, straddling him, my dress riding up in the process.

He eyes me admiringly, his hands on my waist. "I like the new dress I bought you." He smiles.

I roll my eyes. "I don't like you buying me things. It makes me feel guilty," I tell him for the hundredth time since I've met him.

He throws his head back in laughter. "You see my accounts. You know how much money I have."

It's my turn to laugh. "Exactly, Aiden. It's your money. You work so hard for it. Once I get my paycheck, you're not paying for anything anymore."

I mean it.

He brushes it off. "Nonsense. I love," He rubs his long hand down my arm gently, "seeing you in things that my money paid for." He places a kiss on the swell of my breasts peeking out of the dress. "It turns me on."

I bite my lip.

He laughs. "But I'm going to fire all men working here, so they don't stare at you."

I look at him with narrowed eyes, unable to tell if he's joking. "I hope you're playing, because I'll just quit." I smile.

He holds his hands up. "Okay, okay. I'm teasing. But don't you think this is a little short when you're around other guys all day?" He tugs on the fabric.

"You hate it?" I pout, my tone sad.

A half-smile curves his lips. "Actually, it's my favorite. I've been imagining how it'd look on the floor since I saw you this morning." He nibbles on my collarbone.

"I have to get back." My nerves get the better of me, afraid someone may hear.

"Shh, I'm your boss. You do what I say right, Ms. Banks?" His voice is gruff.

I bite my lips. He looks so good, and I've been wanting him all day. "There are people here," I lower my voice to a whisper.

He grips my waist and rocks me against him. Shit.

"Do as I say," He demands, his eyes twinkling.

I gulp when he twists my hair around his hand and pulls me to the floor.

"I want your mouth around me. It's all I could think about all day."

I sit on my knees, hidden underneath his desk. He unzips his pants and pulls himself out. Taking in a deep breath to still my nerves, I lean forward, sucking his already erect cock as he relaxes in his chair. His hand guides my movements.

A knock has me tensing but I continue pleasuring him.

Aiden stiffens. "Busy."

The door clicks open and I lift my head slightly, confused.

Aiden's fingers dig into my hair. He's short of breath, "Ricky? What the fuck man. I said I'm busy."

I hear shoes tapping against the floor, I must have not locked the door properly.

"I know, I know. But I needed your advice." Ricky's tone is pleading.

He isn't going to leave anytime soon.

With the fear of it being another coworker gone, I decide to have a little fun. It's not often I see Aiden squirm. I take in as much of his cock as I can into my mouth without gagging and suck hard, trailing my tongue around his shaft.

He lets out a small moan, gripping my hair tighter. "Go. Ricky." Aiden growls.

"I wanted to take Ashley out, somewhere nice. But I can't think of any place. Please, man."

I continue sucking, humming silently.

Panting, Aiden leans back in his chair. "Emilia is sucking me off under the desk right now."

I stop, surprised. Ricky remains silent before bursting into laughter. I look up at Aiden and see an uneven smile. Fuck, he wins.

"That's my cue."

The door closes and I swat Aiden's leg, scolding lightly, "Why did you tell him?"

He laughs before tugging on my hair, pulling my mouth back to him. He pushes down on the back of my head, forcefully guiding me down his length. He growls. "I knew what you were doing."

I moan.

I love when he takes control. And he always takes control.

"Trying to catch me off guard...I think you forget who's in charge here." He shoves me down and I feel him deep in my throat as he unloads.

Working for Aiden the past couple of weeks has been amazing.

But I've been dreading today.

Meeting my father's killer for the first time.

It's a cool morning. Aiden holds me close, escorting me to the car. I slide into the backseat and Aiden gets in beside me, pulling me tight against him. I have on a very conservative business casual jumpsuit, not wanting Aiden fighting with prisoners while I face my demons.

The loud clanking of metal doors opening and closing echoes throughout the prison. The visitation process passes by in a blur. Muffled sounds close in on me as I wait to walk into the room. I had assumed we'd be behind a glass wall, talking on a phone, like in the movies.

I was wrong.

The officer ushers us into an open room. There are ten tables with chairs surrounding each one. Similar to a small cafeteria. A dad is getting a visit from his wife and children on one side, and on the other, I see a man facing away from us.

Thomas.

Hesitantly, I walk up to the table, using Aiden's arm for support. He slides my chair out and I sit, staring at my hands, too afraid to look up. I wish Mom was here with me, but I didn't dare tell her. She would've flipped.

I look over to make sure Howard is close by. I've rarely seen any emotions on his face, but his eyes are glued to Thomas. His expression is angry, but Aiden...his expression is killer. Animalistic, as he stares down the man who murdered my father.

Now, it's my turn.

I've never seen him in person as I was too scared to go to the court hearings. I saw his blurry mugshot in the paper once, never on the news though... I couldn't bear to look while my mom watched the segments. I expected to see a monster, yet I didn't. Asides from his orange jumpsuit and shackles, he looks...normal.

My hands shake as he looks into my eyes, his expression thoughtful. Aiden taps the table and Thomas's attention snaps to him.

Aiden proceeds to set the rules. "Look down, unless she asks you to look at her. Don't speak, unless she asks you to speak to her. If you make her uncomfortable in any way, I won't hesitate to take you out. Do you understand?" His tone is intimidating.

Thomas bows his head, but I note a smile playing on his lips. His expression is blank when he lifts his head and he doesn't look at me.

I take a deep breath. I had concocted a solid one-sided conversation in my head on the ride here, but now...with him, in front of me, my thoughts are jumbled. I can't put the pieces together.

Deep breaths.

"All I want to say," I pause, gathering my courage. "Look at me." He obeys, his smokey eyes look back at me. "I wanted to let you know that you not only ended my father's life, you ended a lot of other things too."

I sit up straighter, taking courage from Aiden's reassuring hand interlaced with mine. "My mom lost the love of her life, and I don't say that lightly. Their love has no boundaries. My father never got to attend my high school graduation, he never got to send me off to college. He will never get to walk me down the aisle." I choke on my last words and Aiden rubs his thumb along my shaking hand.

Thomas bows his head, looking up when Aiden taps the table in warning, his expression is pained.

It infuriates me.

"I don't know why they're releasing you. You don't deserve to see the light of day again. You'll never have the kind of life my dad lived. You are nothing. No one. A drunk. My father was an honorable man. He was protecting this city, but evil men like you are everywhere. I know what it's like now." He cocks his head to the side. "I know what it's like for your life to be in danger. I've faced men like you. Fuck you."

With that, I burst into tears.

Aiden leans me into his shoulder before gesturing for the guards.

"She's done," He says to Howard.

I nod.

Thomas clears his throat and looks at me. "What do y–"

"Don't you dare fucking speak." Aiden's voice booms through the quiet room.

My eyes are blurry, but I can see Aiden's chest rising and falling as he attempts to calm himself. I've said what I needed to and now, I just want to get out.

I clutch onto Aiden's hand as we make our way to the parking lot. He gets a phone call and lets go of my hand for a moment. Still unbalanced by my emotions and tear-soaked vision, I clumsily trip over my own feet and fall face first onto the pavement. I scream slightly, throwing my hand out to catch myself.

Aiden is by my side in a flash, concern all over his face. "Babe, what happened?"

"I'm clumsy." I shake my head, not wanting to admit that him holding me gives me so much strength and courage that when he let go, I couldn't physically hold myself up any longer. I know I'm a strong girl, but I need him right now. I have no shame in that.

Aiden examines the damage before scooping me up and depositing me in the backseat, snapping at Howard to grab the first aid kit.

"Don't snap at him!" I scold lightly, but Aiden ignores me.

Howard holds out the alcohol and gauze, which Aiden snatches and begins cleaning me up. I pull away and shoot him a look.

"Thank you."

Howard nods, uncomfortable with even the slightest appreciative words.

I let out a small laugh. Even though it's brief, it warms my cheeks.

After I'm cleaned and bandaged – only minor scratches, but I still look beautiful, Aiden claims – he holds me while Howard drives us home.

I'm ready for this shit day to be over.

I had three days off to collect myself, well not completely…I worked at home and got so much more done since Aiden likes to take at least three 'meetings with his assistant' a day. I'm not complaining though.

I feel refreshed. A weight has been lifted from my shoulders. Now, I can focus on healing those pieces that I've held on so vigorously to for so long.

My phone rings.

Aiden's husky voice warms my ears. "Emilia, come into my office a moment."

I happily walk in and smooth my skirt down.

Aiden sits behind his desk, his arm casually draped over the back of his chair. His cuffs are undone. He looks casual yet powerful. He twirls a glass of whiskey, the ice clinking against the crystal, which breaks me from my trance.

"Can I help you with something?" I smile.

"So ready to please." He murmurs, setting down his glass and raking a hand through his styled hair, turning it into an instant perfect mess.

I try not to bite my lip and instead, roll my eyes playfully. "What is it, Aiden?" I tap my heel against the marble tile.

"My maid is sick. Find me a replacement." He looks out of the large windows in thought.

My heart sinks. "I'm so sorry. How long does she have?"

He cocks an eyebrow, studying me in amusement. "What? She's not dying, Emilia. She can't make it in for the rest of the week, so I'm going to fire her. Hire me a replacement."

I scoff. "You're joking right? I won't do it."

He stalks over to me, trailing his long fingers down my top. His hands graze the side of my breast as I try to keep my emotions in check.

"Do I need to remind you who is the boss here? That attitude of yours will get you nowhere here." He smirks.

I step away from him. "Let me clean. She can return next week." I say, with finality in my voice.

He crosses his arms. "I won't allow it."

I groan. "Please, she doesn't deserve to lose her job." I bat my lashes.

He sighs. "Baby, You're mine. I own this company. I won't allow it. Understand?"

I smack his arm. "There's nothing wrong with honest work."

He scans me before glancing out at the empty office. "No. No way are you—"

I give him the best puppy dog eyes I can manage. "No one's here. Let me clean. I'll do it after hours."

"You can start with my office." A slight smirk appears on his features.

I jump up and down before kissing his cheek. Thankful, he didn't argue further but simply closes his door and returns to his desk.

"So, where's the cleaning stuff?"

I open the closet he gestures to, grab a duster and make my rounds around the room. I'm on my tiptoes cleaning a mantel when he chimes in with amusement.

"You missed a spot."

I roll my eyes, not bothering to turn around. "Where, if I may ask."

"The coffee table against the wall below you."

I step back and see that he's right. Armed with a rag, I furiously wipe at the spot. "It won't come off." I groan in frustration.

Aiden laughs. "Move your arm in circles, babe."

I obey. "Like this?"

"Yeah, baby, just like that." A soft moan escapes from his lips.

Puzzled, I turn to see him in his chair, his dress shirt sleeves pulled up, stroking his length. His eyes are on me, caressing the outline of my curves.

I bite my lip at the glorious sight. I tug at my skirt, realizing it rode up at some point. I quickly walk over when he beckons me. He grabs the backs of my thighs, hastily pulling me onto his lap. My feet dangle over the sides of the chair.

"I can't reach."

He laughs. "You're so fucking adorable." He kisses my cheek, his hard length pressed against my slit.

"Isn't this sexual harassment Mr. Scott?" I tease.

He plays with my hair. "You know, I did that once," He murmurs.

I look into his eyes, trying to recall, but I don't remember anything. Sadness rises in me at the thought of him with someone else.

"What's wrong?" He rubs his thumb along my burning skin.

I bury my face in his broad chest, taking a deep breath. "Why would you tell me that?"

His eyebrows knit together. "That I jacked off to you before?"

"You what?" I tilt my head in confusion. "I thought you meant sexual harassment, like hooking up with one of your employees."

He laughs. "No, baby girl. The only employee I would ever touch is you."

I shake my head. "You're lying."

"Don't tell me what I'm doing. If I tell you something, it's the truth. Do you understand? Or do you need me to teach you a lesson?" He playfully takes the strap of my top between his teeth.

"You slept with Rebecca." I remind him.

Realization dawns on his face. "Oh no, baby. She didn't work for me then. I didn't do shit with her after I hired her. I'm smarter than that."

I raise my brow. "Smarter huh? What if I sue you?"

He looks me up and down before smiling wolfishly. "Take everything you want from me. Just let me fuck you."

I shudder at his words. Then, I remember what he said. "What do you mean?" I lower my voice. "That you jacked off to me before. I don't remember that."

"You wouldn't." He caresses my swollen lips. "You were asleep."

I look up at the ceiling in thought.

"You passed out in the car after the incident at the club. I was horny, so I stroked my cock while you slept. You're so obedient when you're not talking." He kisses my bare shoulder. "I didn't touch you."

I believe him. But would I really care if he did? Not at all.

I blush furiously. I know I should be angry or bothered, but I'm not. The thought of him wanting me so badly that he touched himself while I slept turns me on. I can feel myself dripping. I lift up and look down. His cock is glistening. My panties are ruined.

He looks down and smiles. "You like that, huh?"

He pulls my panties to the side, swiping a long finger through my slit. I gasp in pleasure the second he touches my throbbing clit.

"Such a dirty girl. You like the thought of me doing that, don't you?" He rubs faster.

I buck my hips, about to come undone.

His silky voice whispers in my ear, "Not yet. I want to see you bouncing on my cock."

I gesture to my dangling feet with a blush. "I can't reach the floor." I feel so small in his arms, so feminine.

He growls deeply, wrapping a hand around my neck, and brings me close. "I'll just have to bounce you myself."

Aiden yanks my panties further to the side before lifting my hips. He positions me above his length, and I whimper when I feel him pressing against my entrance. I moan as he lowers me, his hard length sliding in and stretching me mercilessly.

"Slower," I beg with a moan.

"No." He chuckles, pushing me down and sinking his length deeper into me.

I wrap my arms around his neck, sinking my fingers into his hair. His hands still on my waist, he lifts me up and down. I sigh in pleasure at the feel of his length filling me, rubbing against my clit. It's heavenly.

Every moment with Aiden is passion filled, euphoric. We're so in tune, it gets better every time. We come undone together, our bodies tangled in his leather chair.

I get dressed, smoothing my hair out so Howard doesn't know what we just did. He's starting to become a father-figure to me.

"So, what time do I need to come in tomorrow to clean?"

He laughs. "You're not cleaning."

"I just did."

"Earlier when you cut me off." He grabs my ass in warning. "I was going to say, just no way are you bending over to clean with the way you look. I'll have to fuck you in the middle of the office ten times a day." He smirks. I turn my face away. "It gave me an idea. I wanted to see you bent over and cleaning for me."

I roll my eyes playfully and swat his arm. "You jerk!"

He shrugs, his perfect half smile melting me. "I love your innocence. But God help whoever tries to fuck with you because you're so gullible. I'll have to kill them.

That spot's been on that table for years, it would've never come off." He laughs.

I playfully hit his arm.

He grabs the material of my skirt, pulling it down. "Am I going to have to go shopping with you to make sure you buy proper clothing?"

"I'll wear whatever I want," I lie with a huff.

He laughs, calling my bluff.

"I only wear it for you," I mutter.

He grips my face possessively when I look away, his voice deep and husky. "Fuck yes, you do, baby girl. Only me."

I blush. "So, I'll hire her a replacement. But only for this week."

He doesn't argue. "Whatever you want."

Twenty-Six

I'm working from home the next few days. Aiden needs to get work done and so do I. We both know we won't be able to keep our hands off each other if I'm in the office, and so we hesitantly parted ways this morning.

I finish all my paperwork early and spend the rest of the day preparing a romantic night with him. Spaghetti Bolognese made from scratch.

A smile crosses his face when Aiden arrives home and sees me in my apron. He takes in a deep breath, enjoying the aromas of a meal that's been simmering for hours. He strides over and I hold the wooden spoon out for him to taste.

"That is fucking delicious," He moans, licking his

lips. I smile at his compliment. "And you look gorgeous." He lingers on the yellow dress he bought me in Brazil.

I twirl with a smile. I knew it would be perfect for tonight. I'm protecting it with an apron, just to be on the safe side but he snickers.

"It's cute."

Noticing his left hand behind his back, I try to peek around, but he moves with me. "What is it?" I giggle.

He presents me with a single yellow rose. The gesture almost brings me to my knees. It would have, if he didn't wrap me in his arms and kiss me fiercely.

My shaking hand grabs the rose sitting in a small vase. I look up at him with pure adoration. "You remembered." A tear rolls down my cheek.

"Of course. You told me when we visited your mom's shop. That story stuck with me." He shrugs casually and looks away.

I can tell he isn't used to doing something so thoughtful. But with me, he always does. I kiss his cheek. "Go get changed, then pour me some red wine."

"Of course, Ms. Banks. Right on it." He nods, wrapping his suit jacket on his arm like a butler before exiting the kitchen.

I place the vase with my single yellow rose on the counter, admiring it while I cook.

Aiden walks in as I take off my apron. Having expected to see him in his gray sweatpants, it warms my heart when I see him dressed up in exactly what I love to see him in for a dinner at home. His dark jeans hang low on his hips, damp black hair tousled atop his head, and a black t-shirt finishes the perfect trio of Aiden.

I did all of this because I have something important to tell him tonight. I want it to be special because he is so special.

Even over the aromatic smells of spaghetti sauce, his heavenly scent overpowers all other smells. My favorite scent in the entire world. Mint with a hint of smoke.

His charming smile ignites a burning desire inside my body. His warm fingers trail the length of my collarbone, his eyes landing on the locket necklace. I smile, knowing how much he loves when I wear his mark. I never take it off, not even to shower.

He leans in closer with a frown. "What happened?" He reaches behind me and unclasps the chain, twirling it in his palm.

A scratch across the front draws my attention. "Must have happened when I fell that day." I pout, angry at myself for being so clumsy. "I'm sorry."

He smiles, shaking his head as he slides the lock in his pocket. "It's fine. I'll get it repaired."

We almost didn't make it through dinner. Aiden's eyes were all over me as I served him his food. Light conversation over candlelight on the patio makes for an insanely romantic setting. The city skyline and the warm glow of the candles had us in a trance. The candlelight flickered against his tan skin, making me melt.

Unable to make it till dessert, we rush up the stairs to the rooftop.

Our rooftop.

Aiden gently lays me down beside him, his jade eyes mesmerizing as he drinks me in. His warm hands are all over me. I want to tell him how much I love his hands on me, how much I love his warm embrace, how much I love him. But I don't.

"You're mine," I groan through ragged breaths.

"As much as you're mine," He replies with a sheepish grin.

I moan as he places a firm hand on my thigh. I smile at him, sinking further into the soft bedding. "This is my favorite part of the apartment. I'm so happy you brought this bed when you moved."

He trails kisses along my stomach. "When I saw the rooftop on this place, I was sold. I knew you'd love it. Plus, I knew the bed I first took you in would fit perfectly up here."

I smile at the memories.

Aiden crawls up the bed, his lips touching mine, his tongue entering my mouth. His body demanding my attention. Then he makes love to me. Soft, gentle and full of passion. My fingers dig into his warm skin as he slides deep into me.

Our bodies tangled underneath the sheets below the city stars. Our lips connect as we reach our peak. Twisting and moaning, hands tangled in each other's bodies, in each other's hair. In each other's souls.

We lay in the twisted sheets, kissing and cuddling.

His phone rings, shattering the moment. With a huff, he hits ignore. But it keeps ringing and ringing.

"What's up?" He spits into the phone, finally picking up. His short temper is evident when it comes to people interrupting his time with me.

I watch his face contort as he jumps off the bed, hastily throwing his pants back on. He stalks to the edge of the building and peeks over the side. Following his lead, I throw my clothes back on. He hangs up. His scowl is gone, replaced with a smooth calm expression when he turns to me, but his eyes are hard.

He takes a step towards me, his expression thoughtful. Pulling me into his arms, he looks down into my eyes as I wrap my arms around his waist.

Worry bubbles up inside me. Something isn't right.

"I'm going to tell you something and I need you to *not* be a stubborn girl." He tilts my chin up. "I need you to listen." He emphasizes the last word.

With the way that his eyes are shining under the moonlight, I can see how serious he is. It's frightening.

"There are some bad men coming."

I gasp, my breath quickening. "Let's go."

He shakes his head. "There's no time, Emilia."

———————

I cry into Aiden's chest as he wraps one arm around my waist and grabs my hand with the other. He hums in my ear, a calm tune, but my heart is beating out of my chest.

It all happens so quickly. I can hear heavy furniture being tossed against the walls downstairs. I don't hear gunshots, but I already know whoever it is, they're using silencers, so the cops don't get called. I cringe, knowing that Howard is down there, in danger. They're searching for us.

"They're going to come for us any minute, Aiden." I gasp.

He pulls me closer.

Why aren't we doing anything?

"Shh, I won't let anything happen to you."

I revel in his embrace. Sighing in defeat, I give up. There's no way out, and I'll be damned if my last moments with him are spent in terror.

He takes his phone out and plays a slow song. Grabbing my hand, he twirls me underneath the starry lights. I follow his fluid and romantic movements in the chaotic mess.

"What are you doing?" I ask through my tears.

"We're slow dancing while they scream."

The sound of heavy boots trekking up the stairs makes tears flow down my cheeks, luckily there's a heavy metal door separating them from us, so we have more time together, and we always lock it when we come up here. This is supposed to be our haven, the one place we don't have to worry about danger.

Aiden pulls me back, studying my face before planting a solitary kiss on my lips. "Come with me," He whispers, placing a hand on the small of my back, guiding me toward the bed.

The bed we first made love on.

In one quick movement, he slides the bed against the concrete carefully, revealing a trap door. He opens the lock and lifts the door, revealing a small underground room.

I shudder in relief. Why did he wait so long?

He lowers me in gently.

"Come on!" I call out when Aiden doesn't follow me down. He simply studies me from above, his emerald eyes drinking me in.

"There's only room for one." He lies.

I know he knows they'll search the place up and down for him and eventually lift the bed.

"Fuck that!" I sob. They're banging on the door; I can hear them.

He holds a finger to his full lips. "Shh, they'll hear you."

I try to think of what to say. Deciding I'm going down with him, I move to crawl out, but he pries my hands from the sides.

"I want to go with you," I tell him, not caring about the consequences.

He can't leave me here like this. My eyes widen at the sight of the padlock in his hands as he brings his hand down.

Aiden blows me a kiss, his voice strong yet loving. "Thank you for you. I'm sorry you have to live without me." He looks behind him, his movements becoming frantic. His voice is calm when he turns back to me one last time. "I love you, Emilia Banks."

"I love you more," I whisper as he closes the heavy door, trapping me inside. I hear the lock click and the bed frame sliding overhead. I want to scream, protest, anything but I don't. It'll cause terror to leak through him and he looked so brave. Fuck.

I swallow my tears, being brave for Aiden as chaos surrounds me.

All I hear is yelling.

Gunfire.

Then, silence.

Epilogue

So, this is how it ends for me.

Aiden closes the door to the hatch, covering up the only serenity he has ever known. His yellow rose. Shielding her as he always has from the horrors of the world.

Through every stage of his life, Aiden's sole focus was material. But now, as the men charge at him with raised weapons, yelling in heavy Italian accents, few things he'd done in his life would matter more than locking his princess away.

She's safe, hidden away from the world.

Nothing else matters to him.

A shot rings out.

He waited for the pain and when it came, he welcomed it. For he was at peace with his demise. Now, they will leave his girl alone, his family and friends alone.

For I, a damned man, will walk through hell for eternity, breathing in the fire of the burning scenery I will endure for endless days. Surrounded by the damned like me.

The thought angered him, as red blood seeped on the cool concrete ground.

She's always with me. When I go, I don't want to bring her, even in thought, to such a wretched place.

As blood pours from his body, a slight pressure builds up against his ribs. Looking through hazed eyes, he sees a set of unfamiliar eyes, waving a gun in his face. Trying to focus his foggy mind, the image in front of him becomes clearer in the chaotic scene.

A man is holding pressure to his wound, clearly irritated as he yells at another unfamiliar stranger beside him. "Cazzo idiota, la sua gamba! Gli ho detto che la sua gamba sanguinerà prima che lo portiamo dove deve andare. Il capo avrà la nostra fottuta testa!"

You fucking idiot, his leg! I said his leg, he'll bleed out before we get him where he needs to go. The boss will have our fucking head!

He scoffs, not worried. Aiden knows where this is going, and it will only end one way. He'll be dead, and order will return to the world. Howard and Ricky know the protocol, so he doesn't need to worry about Emilia looking for him.

The world around him faded in and out of darkness, his body growing heavy. His clock is running out.

He rescued her, traded her life for his.

He may be a damaged knight, but a knight nonetheless in her eyes.

His yellow rose, though sad and alone, will be safe and sound.

Forever.

END OF BOOK ONE

Acknowledgments

First and always, thank you to my Wattpad readers. Your passion for Emden has made this happen! You are the reason this book is published, and I could never properly explain my gratitude for you.

To my wonderful editor, Cheryl Lim. Thank you for always answering my endless emails and for polishing Aiden to perfection while maintaining my writing style. I could never thank you enough! You can learn more about her work here: gwyneiirabookblog.weebly.com

My insanely talented book cover designer, Jessica Scott at UniqueCoversBoutique on Etsy. Your patience and skill created the book cover of my dreams. Thank you for everything you've done for me!

And finally, to my husband who has listened to me talk about fictional characters for hours on end and supported me in following my dreams. I love you more than words.

ALSO BY H.L. SWAN

EMILIA

EMILIA'S SWEET TREATS

GUARDED BY DEATH

HAVEN

RACE TO ME

Printed in Great Britain
by Amazon

62732381R00182